Know the Score

A Vancouver Knights Novel
Book 2

Kylie Kent

ISBN:
Ebook: 978-1-923137-02-8
Paperback: 978-1-923137-21-9

Editing services provided by Kat Pagan:
https://www.facebook.com/PaganProofreading

Club Omerta

Are you a part of the Club?

Don't want to wait for the next book to be released to the public?
Come and join Club Omertà for an all-access pass!

This includes:
• daily chapter reveals
• first to see: everything, covers, teasers, blurbs
• advanced reader copies of every book
• bonus scenes from the characters you love!
• Video chats with me (Kylie Kent)
• and so much more...

Click the link to be inducted to the club!!!
CLUB OMERTA

Foreword

Content warning. This is a dark mafia romance. Please read with caution. Topics found within these pages include but are not limited to: graphic violence, blood, death, and adult language.

Blurb

Kathryn

Everything was perfect until it wasn't. Nobody warns you that it can all be taken away in the blink of an eye.

Now my life revolves around working two part-time jobs to make ends meet while taking care of my daughter alone. Ensuring she doesn't drown in my grief.

When Graycee asks to play hockey, I scrape and save enough to sign her up for the local youth league. The smile on her face as she steps out onto the ice makes every sacrifice worth it.

It's the same smile I used to see on her father whenever he played too. The smile that still haunts me to this day. The one I never thought I'd see again in person.

But somehow those dark eyes and that cocky-as-shit smirk are staring right back at me. Grayson Monroe, the man I've been hiding from in plain sight for the last six years.

Grayson

I didn't want to believe it at first. Kathryn Kilgor, a girl I never thought I'd see again. She's here. In this rundown skating rink, meant to host Vancouver's next generation of hockey players.

I searched for this woman for years and couldn't find her. Now that I have, I realize she's not alone. She has a daughter. A little girl, with the same set of dark eyes that look back at me every time I stare into a mirror.

Still, I don't want to believe that Kathryn would do this. She wouldn't hide a child from me, my child from me. I gave this woman everything. My heart, my soul, my fucking dignity. And she stepped on it like it was worth nothing.

The panic on her face shouldn't excite me. But I've been hurting for six years now, all because of her. I'm thinking it's time my runaway ex felt some of that pain too.

To Kathryn,

Thank you for being you. I'm so blessed to have you on this journey with me. Your generosity and kindness know no bounds. You truly are an inspiration. I appreciate you for being you, even all the wonderfully odd and unusual parts.

Xx,

Kylie

Chapter One

Six Years Earlier

The sound of the crowd gets my blood pumping. This is what I fucking live for. The coldness of the ice, the feel of the stick in my hand, the blaring of the horns, the music booming from the speakers, the smoke and lights flashing. This DJ has his art nailed down.

"Seek and Destroy" by Metallica thunders through the rink as my skates hit the ice. I fucking love everything about hockey. Live and breathe it. But what I love more than anything else is the moment I step onto the ice and I see her. Kathryn Kilgor, the only person who's managed to take over more of my soul than this game.

She jumps up and spins around. Something she does every game to show off the words on the back of her jersey. Monroe. My name. I smile when she turns back around and waves at me. Kathryn loves the sport just as much as I do, which I honestly didn't think was possible.

The sound of my name being chanted fills the rink as the team warms up. Just before it's time to skate off the ice again, I breeze over to where Kathryn is seated and touch my glove to the plexiglass. She pushes to her feet and does the same, mouthing the words "kick ass" to me.

"You're pussy-whipped as fuck, dude." My teammate shakes his head in disgust.

"Jealousy isn't a color that looks good on you, Westin." I laugh at him.

"Jealous? Of only putting my dick into one hole? Hard fucking pass," he grunts.

I ignore the dumbass. I don't give a fuck what anyone thinks. They don't know what Kathryn and I have. They're the ones missing out, if you ask me.

Westin's just been signed to the NHL. This is his last year with us and my eye is on his current position on our college team. Right now, I wear the A. But it's the C I want. Team Captain. And when I want something, I don't ever fucking stop until I get it.

"Let's get out there and fucking win," the coach shouts.

I take my place with my teammates, preparing to walk back down the tunnel. And, again, that feeling hits me as I step out onto the ice with my line. I skate over to my position and eye the opposing team. The fucking Columbian Thunderbirds. They're decent enough, but not as good as we are. They know it too, judging by the hardened glares on their faces.

They're ready to do whatever it takes to try to win. They know they won't, but they gotta at least try, right?

The puck drops, and all my focus is on that round disk. Westin sends it flying down the ice, and I'm charging after it, knocking right into the fucker attempting to block me. I get to the puck, rush the crease, and aim for the back of the net.

I raise my stick in the air as my teammates pile up on me, celebrating the first goal of the game within the first minute. It's a great fucking feeling. My gaze flicks over to Kathryn. She's on her feet, screaming and jumping up and down. Having someone in your corner, that unconditional support and love... I never expected to find it, let alone at such a young fucking age. But I knew. The first time I saw her across the cafeteria two years ago, I fucking knew.

"Chug, chug, chug, chug!" Everyone around me chants as I down the beer in one go.

When I come up for air, my arm wraps around Kathryn, pulling her tight against me, and my mouth slams onto hers. She returns my kiss for a second before pulling away and scrunching up her face. "Gross, what the hell did you just drink?"

"No idea." I smirk. "But I know what I wanna drink." I raise my eyebrows up and down at her suggestively.

"Really, Gray? You think these guys are going to let their star player bail from the party?" She laughs.

"Who said anything about bailing?" Taking hold of her hand, I navigate around the crowd—technically, they all move the fuck out of my way without me having to say a word—while tugging Kathryn around the nearest corner.

This hockey frat house is like my second home. I say second because I have my own apartment off campus. I do spend a lot of time here, though. Which is great because it means I know the fastest route to the one spot I know no one will be presently occupying. The guys refer to it as the trophy room. Basically, it's a living room filled with pictures and memorabilia from the team's former players. The greats. I'm still waiting for my jersey to be framed and put on this wall. It'll happen before I graduate. That much I'm sure of.

This room stays under lock and key during parties. Some of the shit in here would sell for a small fortune. Entering the code, I pull Kathryn inside and slam the door shut. It takes less than a minute for me to pick her up and drop her onto the sofa. Another minute and I'm on my knees in front of her.

Kathryn's laughter drowns out the muffled sounds of the party blaring on the other side of these walls. Gripping each of her thighs, I spread her legs open as wide as her denim skirt allows them to go.

"Mmm, you taste much better than anything I've ever eaten." I lick and suck my way up her thigh.

Kathryn shimmies her skirt up over her hips, spreading her legs wider for me. "I think you should probably try more. Just to make sure, you know?" Her cheeks blush as she looks down at me.

"Have I told you how brilliant you are? I think that idea alone is worthy of a Nobel Prize." My teeth bite into the soft flesh of her upper thigh. I pull her panties to the side, and as slowly as I possibly can, I run my tongue up the middle of her slit.

"Oh shit, Gray." Kathryn's hands land on the top of my head, her fingers tangling through my hair. She pushes my face into her mound harder.

I growl as I latch on to her clit and suck. Her taste explodes on my tongue. No matter how hard I suck, how much I lick at her, it's not enough. I need more. I eat her out like she's my first meal of the day.

When you train as much as I do, your body requires higher volumes of food. Though I'm not sure the dietician was referring to my girlfriend's cunt when he told me to increase my caloric intake. But that's exactly what I took from it.

My right hand shifts and I push two fingers inside her. She's so fucking wet her juices run down my hand.

"Oh, fuck!" Kathryn's thighs shake, and I have to put extra weight on her to keep her pinned to the sofa.

Her cunt tightens, and I don't stop when her orgasm begins to ebb away. No, I double-down my efforts and relish the reward as a second orgasm rolls through her. Then I kiss my way up her body until I get to her mouth, slamming my lips onto hers. Kathryn wraps her arms and legs around me, pushing her pussy into my groin. My cock is rock hard and begging to be let free.

"I need you, Gray," Kathryn moans.

"You have me. All of me," I tell her. I pick her up and then sit us on the sofa with her legs straddling my lap. "Take out my cock."

I watch as Kathryn's hands fumble with my belt and then the button on my jeans. She's eager. She always is. Two years. We've been fucking each other for two years now. Since she was a freshman. I'm not sure there's a position we haven't tried out. And yet, no matter how much we fuck, every time is just as good as the first.

No, that's a lie. Every time is fucking better.

Kathryn's hand wraps around my dick. She pulls it out of my briefs and stares while licking her lips. Fuck, that mouth of hers always feels good wrapped around me. But her cunt is better.

"Sit yourself on my cock, babe. I want to feel your pussy choke the fuck out of me," I tell her. She nods her head and rises onto her knees. I help hold her panties out of the way as she sinks herself down on me. Slowly.

"Oh god! Shit, Gray." Kathryn throws her head back as her mouth parts on a moan. "How does it always feel this good?"

"It's you, babe. You do this," I tell her, lifting my hips and burying myself deeper into her. "All of this is because of you." My left hand moves from her hips, underneath the inside of her jersey, cupping her tit and rolling her nipple through my fingertips. "You make me so fucking hard, Kathryn. Only you." My right hand wraps around her throat, forcing her to look at me. "Ride me. Make yourself come on my cock. Let me feel that cunt of yours quiver."

Kathryn's only response is a moan. Her hips lift up and slam back down. She grinds her clit onto my pelvis and repeats the process. "You feel... oh god... I need..."

"Take whatever you need, babe. It's yours," I tell her.

She grabs my hand and adds pressure to my hold on her throat. I wasn't squeezing hard enough, it seems. I tighten my grip until her airway is blocked, counting to ten in my head before backing off for a few seconds and repeating the process. Her hips grind down on me and her juices drench my lap. A silent scream leaves her mouth as she comes, her pussy milking my cock for everything I have.

I already told her it's all hers.

I drop my hand from her throat and pull her down so her head is on my shoulder. My arms close around her back, holding her to me like the prized possession she is. "I love you," I tell her.

"I love you so much, Gray," she rasps.

"Good. Even if you didn't, I wouldn't let you go," I say. Because it's the fucking truth. If this girl tried to leave me, there is no telling the lengths I'd be prepared to go to in order to find her. Keep her.

"I'll always love you," Kathryn says, pulling back

to look at me. "Promise me you'll always remember that. Never, ever doubt that I love you, Gray."

There've been times over the last few years when she's made me promise this same thing. To never forget how much she loves me. I'm not sure what has her thinking I could. I've done everything I can think of to let her know how serious I am about her.

Fuck, I'm the only guy on the fucking team with a girlfriend. I hear shit about it every day in the locker room. How pussy-whipped I am. I don't care, though, because it's fucking true. I *am* pussy-whipped and Kathryn's the one holding the other end of that whip.

"Promise me, Gray. You have to," she urges again.

"I promise I'll never forget that you love me," I tell her. "Not even when I'm old and lose my memory and shit. The one thing I will always remember is that you love me, Kathryn."

How could I not know? She shows me every day.

"Thank you." She sighs and relaxes against me. "Should we go back out there? You think they're looking for you yet?" she asks.

"Nah, I'm content right here. Screw 'em. Let 'em look for me."

"Your friends already hate me enough, Gray. If

they think I've taken you away from another party, they'll hate me even more."

"They don't hate you. They're jealous because they can't fucking have you. No one can have you, because you're mine," I tell her.

Chapter Two

I try to roll out of bed as stealthily as I can. It's no use. Gray stirs awake the moment I slip out from under his arm. "Where do you think you're going?" he mumbles.

"Shh, go back to sleep. I have to go meet Lil for breakfast. I promised her," I tell him.

"I can't sleep without you in bed. You know that," he grumbles and pushes himself up.

I stand there and stare. Dumbstruck. Like a deer caught in the headlights. Or maybe more like someone appreciating a fine piece of art, because that's what Grayson's body is. Freaking art. All those lines and smooth muscle. I've tried to memorize every inch of him, just to have those images locked away for a rainy day.

"Sorry." I shake my head to clear the Grayson fog. That's what I've come to call the spell he puts on me.

The smirk that flutters across his overly hand-some face tells me he knows exactly where my mind just went. "You know, you could jump back into bed and we can tick off morning cardio."

"That's tempting," I say and mean every word. "But Lil is going home today, and I won't see her until our break's over, so I need to meet up with her for breakfast."

"Fine, but I get you for lunch and dinner and dessert," Gray mutters under his breath.

"Grayson, I'm going home with you tomorrow. Which means you will have my undivided attention for every meal." I lean down and press my lips to his. "Stop pouting. It's not cute." I grin at his scowl.

"It works so well when you do it. Figured it's got to work on you eventually." He pouts harder—if that's possible.

"Oh, it works. I just have more willpower than you do."

"You coming back? When you finish breakfast?" he asks me.

"I have to go to my dorm and pack, and then I have to return some books to the library. How about we meet for dinner?" I suggest.

Gray's mouth drops open. "You're going to make me wait a whole day? That's so cruel, like the meanest thing anyone has ever done to me," he says.

"I doubt anyone has ever been mean to you, Grayson. You're adored way too much. Plus, your family is scary." I laugh.

It's not a lie. Grayson is the most-loved guy on this campus. At first, I thought it was out of fear. I thought everyone was just super nice to him because of who his father is. You know, because he's the son of Jacob Monroe, Canada's version of the Godfather.

And then I got to know him and realized it was hard not to love the guy.

Gray doesn't take *no* for an answer. His persistence is what made me cave into temptation. For the first few weeks, he kept finding ways to "accidentally" run into me on campus. Then he'd ask me out, and I'd declined him every time, until he mentioned going skating.

I mean, how could I say no to that? A date at the rink. With the school's hottest new hockey star at that. I couldn't. And it wasn't that body of his that looks like it's carved out of marble or those green eyes that remind me of dark emerald stones that had me caving. It wasn't even the dimples he gets whenever he smiles.

Nope, it was the idea of getting out on the ice.

Something no one really knows about me is how much I love hockey. Everything about the game, the brutality of it, the players flying down the ice. All of it. When I was little, I wanted to play hockey more than anything else. But my dad would never let me. He always said hockey wasn't a sport for little girls and forced me to do figure skating instead. I hated figure skating, but I loved being on the ice, so I kept going to classes. I competed and I even won a few trophies. I stopped after high school. No one knows about that embarrassing time in my life when I used to dress up in flashy outfits and do figure eights. Not even Gray.

He knows I can skate, obviously. He just doesn't know where or how I learned to do it. I told him my parents took me to the public skating rink as often as they could, and I just picked it up. It's actually one of my favorite things to do with him now. He takes me skating as often as he can. There is something freeing about being out on the ice with him. But maybe that's just Gray. When I'm with him, I feel like there's nothing in this world that can touch me. Nothing that can hurt me.

It's a false sense of security. I know that. I'm not naïve. I don't put too much thought into that feeling. Well, no more than a few minutes at a time.

When I walk into the café, Liliana is already waiting for me. She's even ordered my go-to breakfast. A green smoothie and a chocolate croissant. In my mind, the healthiness of the smoothie counteracts the *un*healthiness of the fatty pastry.

"I'm sorry I'm late," I say, wrapping my arms around my best friend's neck. "Again." I sigh.

"It's fine. If I had a hockey hunk in my bed every morning, I'd be late too." She grins.

I laugh as my eyes flick around the café. Then I pull out the chair, sit down, and check over my shoulder again.

"What are you looking for?" Lil asks.

"Your father's goons. Just waiting for them to

jump out with the chastity belt," I deadpan, and Liliana rolls her eyes.

"Shut up. It's not funny," she huffs.

"It kind of is." I shrug.

Liliana Valentino has been my best friend since the first day of college when I found her hiding out in the girls bathroom. She looked like she'd rather be anywhere else. I remember asking her what she was hiding from, only to laugh when she told me it was her father and his inability to let go.

It wasn't until a few weeks later that I learned who her father was. Theo Valentino, the underboss of the Valentino Crime Family. I knew who the Valentinos were, of course. And what they were— *still are*—is a group of people I would never fuck with. Just like Gray's family. The Monroes. I wouldn't want to get on their bad side either.

It's ironic for someone like me to end up best friends with a mafia princess while dating a mafia prince. Sometimes I wait for the hidden cameras to jump out and a TV show host to inform me I'm being punked. But that's not the only thing that has me on edge lately. There's also a huge secret I've been hiding from both of them. Something I can't tell them or ever let them find out about me. Which is why I've been especially careful. Made sure no one else knows what I've done, what I'll continue to do to be able to stay in school.

I keep telling myself that once I graduate and get a job, I'll move on with my life. That I won't ever have to hack into someone else's bank account and steal from them again.

I know what you're thinking. I'm a terrible person. And you're right. I am.

But I don't steal from just anyone, only from those who get their money the same way, through illegal operations. And I'm careful, taking small sums here and there. Such a miniscule amount that no one notices. I've never taken from Liliana's or Gray's family though. I wouldn't do that to them. I need to be able to look them in the faces, if my secret were to ever get out. Even if all I saw staring back at me was disappointment.

Both Liliana and Gray think I'm here on a full scholarship. It's the reason I tell them I spend so much time in the library studying. Because if I let my grades drop, I'll lose my funding and I can't afford to let that happen. As far as I know, they believe me. Which is just another reason I feel guilty.

"Kathryn, you here or somewhere else? Oh god, please don't tell me you're thinking about your boyfriend while you're sitting here with me." Lil's voice breaks me out of my own head.

"Sorry, no. I'm just... stressing about having to meet his family," I tell her.

"Why?"

"Because they're... well, you know who they are. It's kind of intimidating."

"You've been home with me before. You've met my family," she says. That's true. We've all intermingled on more than one occasion. Her father is friends with Gray's dad.

"That's not the same. I'm not dating your family's prized child," I remind her.

"Well, you'd have to like girls for that to happen *and* be into someone a few years younger. God help whoever ends up dating Tilly." Liliana laughs.

Tilly is her younger cousin, and my best friend insists the girl is the family's favorite. But I've seen how much Liliana's parents love her, so I'm not buying that whole *golden child* thing.

"I think I'll stick with Gray." I smile.

"Good choice. So when are you leaving?"

"Tomorrow morning." I sigh. "What if they hate me, Lil?"

"I'll have my dad put a hit out on them," she deadpans.

"I can't tell if you're serious or not. So, I'm going to assume you're not."

"You know what they say about making assumptions." She laughs.

"Yeah, it makes an ass out of you and me."

"Yep, and we..." Liliana points between the two of us. "...are not asses."

"What are your plans during the break?" I ask, quickly changing the subject.

"Mmm, to shop and spend as much of my dad's money as I can. And then maybe shop some more." She shrugs. "And find a way to dodge his goons so I can actually get laid."

"Good luck with that," I tell her. "Although you could just screw one of the goons. It's not like they're ugly," I suggest. I've seen the men who work for her father, and they sure are easy on the eyes.

"I could, but that would be like signing their death certificates myself, and I can't live with that on my conscience," she says. "Surprisingly enough, I actually have one of those."

I'm not too sure I do. If I did, I'd probably feel bad about the things I've done. The money I've stolen from people.

After breakfast, I head back to my dorm room, collect my laptop, and then go to the library. Because it has the best Wi-Fi signal on campus. The software I use to redirect my location needs a decent connection. If the signal drops for even a second, the masking software will drop with it, and then my IP address will be visible to anyone who's looking.

I fire up the screen and start coding. It doesn't take long, and I don't need much, just enough to cover next semester's tuition. Five minutes later, I'm done and quickly close everything down.

I walk out of the library right into a solid brick wall of muscle. Gray's hands wrap around me. "Whoa, where's the fire? You in a rush to get somewhere?" he asks me.

"Yeah, my boyfriend gets needy and impatient. If I don't get back to him soon, he's likely to come hunt me down." I smile up at him.

"Sounds like a keeper, that one," he says with a grin.

"He is, for sure." I push up on my tiptoes and press my lips to his.

"You get your books returned?"

"Uh-huh. Now, come on, I still need to pack some clothes for the break."

"Or you could spend the entire time naked." Gray lifts a suggestive brow.

I frown at him. "You want me to meet your dad and your siblings naked?"

"Fuck no. I want you in my bed naked. For the whole two weeks."

"Okay, but I still need clothes. For those odd times when we have to come up for air."

"Yeah, probably a good idea." Gray takes my bag off my shoulder and puts it over his before he entwines his fingers with mine. "I'm really glad you're finally letting me take you home."

"Me too." I smile, even though I'm nervous as hell.

I love him. I want his family to like me. He speaks so highly about them, and I can tell he misses them when he's here. But then, whenever he goes home to visit, he spends the whole time telling me how much he wishes I was there with him. And I really do want him to have the best of both worlds. I want him to be happy.

Chapter Three

Grayson

Kathryn's hand shakes in mine as we disembark from the jet. She's been nervous the whole flight over. I thought it was just the flying that had her on edge, but I think it's the whole *meeting the family* thing that's got her on high alert.

She doesn't need to be worried, though. Because they're going to love her. How could they not? The girl is fucking loveable.

"It's going to be okay, babe. Really. Stop stressing," I tell her.

"Easy for you to say. You're not the one meeting the family of your boyfriend of two years."

"They're going to love you, and if they don't, who fucking cares? *I* love you, and that's all that matters." I pick up our joined hands and kiss her knuckles.

"I love you. I just really want them to like me, Gray," she says.

"Come on." I open the back door of the waiting SUV, where my dad's driver is sitting behind the wheel.

"Grayson, welcome home." John nods in my direction.

"Thanks, John. It's good to be home," I say.

"So, this is the famous Kathryn, huh? It's a pleasure to finally meet you, ma'am." John smiles at me.

"Thank you, and you can call me Kathryn, not ma'am," she replies.

John nods his head, but he won't call her Kathryn. He's way too old school for that.

Half an hour later, the car pulls into my father's estate, and Kathryn looks like she's ready to throw up. Holding her hand tighter, I step out of the SUV with her following close behind me.

I hear a squeal and then my name is yelled out. I drop Kathryn's hand to catch my little sister as she leaps into my arms.

"Lia, shit, are you trying to knock me out?" I say, squeezing her a little too tight. It's been way too long since I've seen her, and I swear every time that I do, she just gets more fucking grown up. Which I hate, of course.

My little sister is going to be starting college not long after I graduate, which means it'll be another four years of only seeing her on breaks. Another four years of me not being around full time to keep the assholes at bay.

Aliyah looks like our mother used to. Fucking beautiful. Too bad the outside was the only thing appealing about the woman. Not my sister, though. No, this girl is beautiful inside and out.

"One of these days, I will," Lia says. "Now, let me go." Then she pushes away from me. "Hi, I'm Aliyah, the little sister. Gray has been talking about you nonstop. He said you were pretty. You are."

"Okay, Lia, that's enough," I grunt, cutting her off before she has a chance to spill all my secrets.

"Hi, he talks about you a lot too." Kathryn smiles.

"I know. He's obsessed with me." Aliyah laughs. "Come on, I'll give you the tour."

"Lia, where's Dad?" I ask her.

"In his office, where he always is."

"Great, how about you go and tell him we're here? And I'll show Kathryn around," I tell her.

"Fine, but I want time with her too, Gray. You can't hog her." My sister crosses her arms over her chest. "I've wanted a sister my whole life. And now I get one," she says and then turns around and sprints back the way she came.

"Sorry. She's a little much." I take Kathryn's hand and lead her inside the house.

"It's okay," Kathryn says.

"Trust me, babe, after the next two weeks, you're going to be thankful you're an only child," I tell her.

"I heard that." Vinny is walking down the stairs as we start making our way up to the second floor.

"I stand by my words." I wrap my arms around my little brother. "How you been?"

"Good. You?" he asks.

"Can't complain." I smile at Kathryn. "Vinny, this is Kathryn. Kathryn, Vinny." I wave a hand between them in introduction.

"Hey." Vinny gives her one of his trademark smirks, and I slap him upside the head.

"No," I tell him.

"Ow, what the hell, Gray?"

"Don't look at my girlfriend like that," I grunt at him.

"Like what?" he asks.

"Like you like what you see," I grind out.

"So you want me to pretend she's ugly? Got it." He laughs and then turns to Kathryn. "It's good to have you here. This one has been a grouch the last few times he's been home."

"Thank you. I'm sorry you had to put up with him like that," Kathryn says.

"Catch ya later, bro. People to see and people to do," Vinny calls out over his shoulder as he runs down the stairs.

I take Kathryn into my bedroom and close the door. She steps inside and sits on the bed before standing back up. She's quiet as she looks around, picking up the occasional trophy and shit from the shelves that line one of my walls.

"You okay?" I ask her.

"Mmm. So this is where you grew up into you?" She smiles. "It's very... *you*."

"What does that mean? Very me?"

"I don't know. The room just... it suits you. It's masculine, but also homey and welcoming. It feels...

safe," she says.

"You know you're always safe with me, Kathryn. I'd die before I ever let anything hurt you," I tell her.

"I know. But you dying... something hurting you would be the worst thing that could happen to me. So don't go doing that."

"Not planning on it."

"Good." She grins at me.

"I have plans. *We* have plans."

"The Stanley Cup kind of plans," she says.

"Exactly. I'm going to make it to the NHL. I'm going to win that Cup, and you and I are going to drink from it. Together."

"Not really sure how you're going to make all that happen, but if anyone can do it, I'm sure it's you, Grayson," she says.

"I really love that you're here," I tell her. "You have no idea how many times I've fantasized about fucking you on this bed." I reach a hand over and flick the lock into place on my door.

Kathryn steps backwards until her knees touch the bed. She sits down and runs her hand over the comforter. "This bed?"

I nod my head, slowly approaching her while stripping out of my clothes.

"What did we do in these fantasies of yours, Gray?" she asks me.

"So many things. Filthy, dirty things. Things I'd much rather show you than tell you."

"So show me then," she says.

"Stand up." I stop right in front of her. When she's on her feet, I instruct her to strip.

Kathryn's so fucking obedient. She never questions anything I tell her to do in the bedroom. She just does it, without hesitation. But as she reaches for the hem of her sweater, there's a knock on the door.

"Gray, Dad said to tell you to come out of your room. Dinner is ready," Aliyah yells from the other side.

"Coming," I call back to my sister. "Or at least I wish I was," I grumble under my breath.

"Come on, we have plenty of time to play out your fantasies," Kathryn says while straightening her clothes.

I put my shirt back on, open the door, and half expect to find Aliyah standing there waiting for us, but she's gone.

When we enter the dining room a few minutes later, everyone is already seated around the table. "Dad, this is Kathryn," I say, pulling out a chair for her to sit. "Kathryn, Dad. But you can call him Jacob."

"Kathryn, it's nice to finally meet you." Dad smiles at her.

"You too, Mr. Mon—I mean, Jacob. I've heard so much about you." Kathryn's nerves show in her voice and the way it shakes when she speaks.

Dad raises an eyebrow at her. "Don't believe any of it."

"I'm Jonah," my brother chimes in.

"You're studying business, right?" Kathryn asks him.

"Yep, I'm the smart one." Jonah smiles proudly at his self-proclaimed title.

"Ah, not true. I'm smarter than all three of you combined." Aliyah's voice is high-pitched as she raises it to a level loud enough for the whole house to hear her.

Kathryn looks at me. She has no idea what to do. I sit next to her and take hold of her hand. My family is a lot. That's just something she'll have to get used to. "How's school, Aliyah?" I ask my sister.

"Good, I got the head cheer spot." She beams.

My teeth grind together. My little sister on the cheer team is not something I ever wanted to happen. I've been an athlete my whole life, which means I know exactly what those boys do with the cheerleaders. "Dad, you can't seriously be letting her do that."

"Why wouldn't I let her?" he asks me.

"Because cheerleaders walk around school in barely any clothes and the guys all only have one thing on their minds when they look at them. Especially the athletes. I'm not letting my sister become no puck bunny," I growl.

"Relax. No one is touching your sister," Dad says.

"How do you know?" I challenge him.

"Because she's my daughter. That's how I know. You really think I'm going to let some punk get close enough to touch her?"

"You didn't know every time I..." Shit. I snap my mouth shut.

I wanted to say *every time I fucked a girl in the locker room at that same school.* But I can't say that with Kathryn sitting next to me. I mean, she knows I was no saint before I met her, but I'm not about to rub that fact in her face. She knows exactly what I was going to say too. I look at her and see her biting her lip, trying not to smile.

"Every time you what?" Aliyah asks.

"None of your business. Just quit the cheer squad. You don't even like cheerleading," I tell her.

"I don't. But it looks good on my college applications." She shrugs.

"Your last name alone will get you into any fucking school you want," I'm quick to remind her.

"Language," Dad grunts.

The rest of dinner goes much the same. Me trying to get Aliyah to quit cheerleading, and my sister refusing to listen to reason. Needing to get out of the house after all this back-and-forth bullshit, I tell my dad I'm going to show Kathryn the sights.

I think we drive around for about ten minutes before we end up at The Castle. Home of the Vancouver Knights, the hockey team my father owns. The same team I'm hoping to get drafted into. You'd think it was a sure bet, considering who my dad is, but that's not how it works. My father might have sway when it comes to who he signs, but he sure as fuck won't sign someone who won't win him games.

Kathryn finishes tying up her laces and looks up at me. "Are you sure it's okay for us to be here?"

"We own this place, babe. It's fine." I hold out a hand for her to take.

41

"Still... this is the Knights' arena, Gray. It's huge," she says.

We step out onto the ice together and she lets go of my hand, running out to the middle of the rink where she twirls around in a circle.

"You know, this is where it's going to happen. Where we're going to be holding that Cup," I tell her.

"Where *you're* going to be holding that Cup. I'll be in the stands. Probably pregnant or with an armful of your already-born babies." She smiles.

I freeze. We haven't discussed having kids before. "You want to have my babies, Kathryn?" I ask her.

"I don't want any babies if they're not yours, Gray. I want a little girl with your green eyes. We'll name her Graycee, and I already know she's going to be a huge daddy's girl."

"Graycee. I like it. And when we have a son, what will *his* name be?"

"Hmm, maybe Jacob, after your dad." Kathryn nods as though it's a done deal.

"I like that too. Can we practice the whole *me getting you knocked up* thing now?" I ask her.

"Right now, no. Because I am not wasting my once-in-a-lifetime opportunity to skate around this rink," she says. "Come on. Come dance with me." Kathryn holds out her hands while gesturing for me to join her.

Dancing on the ice with this girl is one of my favorite pastimes. I'd never admit this to anyone, but I'd rather be spinning around with Kathryn than doing just about anything else in the world.

Chapter Four

Kathryn

W hy am I nervous? I've been with Grayson for two years now. And here I am, sitting on his bed in the room he grew up in, waiting for him to get out of the shower. This isn't anything I haven't done a million times before. I practically live at Gray's place. He keeps telling me that he can't sleep without me in bed with him, and considering his apartment and mattress are so much nicer than my cramped dorm room, that's where we tend to be every night.

Gray walks out of the bathroom. Steam billows out of the doorway behind him. My eyes run up and down his body. Transfixed. Completely in awe of the fact that this man, this beautiful god of a man, happens to be mine.

"See something you like?" Gray asks while holding his cock in his hand, slowly stroking it up and down.

I nod my head. "Something I like a lot. Something I want right now," I tell him.

Gray walks over to the bed. My eyes stay focused on his cock *and* the hand that's wrapped around it. My mouth waters while the heat in his eyes lights up my entire body. No one has the effect on me that this man does. Just one look, one smile, and I'm nothing but a melting puddle of tingling nerves.

"Lie across the bed," he instructs.

I shift myself up and do as I'm told. I don't know what he has in store for me. But I do know, whatever it is, I'm in for a hell of a good time.

"You're so fucking perfect," Gray says, leaning over the bed. He grabs hold of my arms, raising them over my head and then he pulls, dragging my body along the mattress until my neck bends over the edge. "Open your mouth." His voice is coming out raspy now.

I quiver, licking my lips before I comply.

"Wider," he says, stroking his cock and running the tip of it along my bottom lip.

And I do, eager to have him in my mouth. My tongue darts out and licks down the tip of his cock, collecting the precum that's leaking freely now.

"So fucking good," Gray says while leaning over me. He rests the tip of his cock between my lips. "Suck me, Kathryn. I want to feel the back of your throat. Take me all the way."

I close my lips around him and suck as he slides down my throat. At this angle, he goes much deeper. I groan and clamp my hands on the back of his thighs, holding him in place. I don't want to stop this anytime soon. Gray continues to slide his cock in and out of my mouth as I lick and suck. His speed picks up, and I double down on my efforts, hollowing out my cheeks as I do.

"Fuck! Yes. Fuck, your mouth feels so good, babe." Gray's legs begin to shake. He's close to coming. I can feel it. "You're going to take it all, Kathryn. You're going to swallow every drop I feed you," he grunts, his movements becoming more rigid.

I nod my head as much as I can, agreeing to do just that. I lift a hand from his leg. My fingers find my clit and I start rubbing. I'm so turned on it doesn't take long for me to find the edge of my own release.

"Holy shit, make yourself come. Come with me, babe. Now," Gray groans as the first squirt of his seed shoots down my throat.

My thighs tighten, my fingers press down harder on my clit, and I follow him right into that orgasm. I'm not sure there's an order Gray could give me that I'd be able to refuse. Well, not in the bedroom anyway.

He pulls his cock out of my mouth and picks me up before throwing me back down onto the bed, higher up so that my head lands on the pillows this time. Then Gray climbs on top of me, covering my body with his.

"That was just the beginning, babe." He smirks at me.

I wrap my arms around his neck and pull his lips onto mine. This is going to be one hell of a night if the start is anything to go by.

"Where did you get to?" Gray asks when I walk through the front door of his family's home.

I swallow the lump in my throat. I don't know if I can do this, but I know I need to. This is for him. As much as it hurts, I know what I have to do. I suck in a breath.

"I have to go home. I'm sorry. I just got a call from my mom. She needs me to help her with my grandmother," I tell him.

"Okay, no problem. We can help your mom," Gray says. "I'll just get dressed—"

"No," I respond a little too quickly. "Sorry... I just... my mom hasn't met you yet, Gray, and she's not in a good way. This isn't the best time for you to come home with me. I'm just gonna go spend the night with her, and I'll come back tomorrow," I tell him.

"Let me at least drive you." His eyebrows knit together as he rubs at the back of his neck. He's concerned. And it's killing me.

"Gray, I appreciate that, but I've already called an Uber to come get me. Just hang out with your brothers and sister. It's one day, one night really, and I'll be back before you know it." I wrap my arms around his neck and press my lips to his.

I have to keep it in the back of my head that this is for him. I can't be selfish right now. I don't think I've ever loved anyone like I love this man. There isn't anything I wouldn't do for him, even if it costs me *everything*... He's my priority.

"Okay, but just so you know, I'd much rather hang out with you than with my siblings."

"I know." I drop my hands and step away. "I'll call you tonight," I tell him before walking backwards towards the door.

"I love you," he says.

I'm fighting the tears. I can't cry in front of him right now. He will know something is wrong.

"I know. I love you too, more than anything else in the entire world. Don't forget that. Promise," I remind him.

"I'll never forget, Kathryn."

I turn around and walk out the door. It's not until

I make it through the gates and down the street that I finally let the tears fall. Then I bend over in someone's perfectly manicured garden and throw up, my stomach repulsed by what I've done. What I'm *doing*.

I pull out my phone and call the one person I know who can help me. Who will do it without question.

"Hey, missing me already?"

"Liliana, I need you. Your help. I'm on my way to New York but you can't tell anyone. And if anyone asks, you haven't heard from me," I say in one long breath.

"Okay, send me your flight details. I'll meet you at the airport," she replies, then adds, "Kathryn, whatever happened, we can fix it, okay? I'll help you."

"Thank you. I'll see you soon." I hang up before I break down completely.

Everything in me wants to turn around, go back into that house, and tell Gray I've made a terrible mistake. I can't do that, though.

The Uber pulls up in front of me and I get in. I send Liliana a message with my flight information and then take the sim card out of my phone and throw it out the car window.

This is it. There is no going back. Because I love him too much to go back.

Chapter Five

Grayson

"Fuck!" I throw my phone against the wall of my bedroom. It's just a little past midnight. I've been calling Kathryn for the last three hours. She said she'd call. She always calls. Something is wrong. I feel it in my gut. I knew I shouldn't have let her leave without me. I don't know what I was thinking. She didn't look well. I thought she was just upset about her grandmother. But now I'm not so sure.

My bedroom door swings open. "Why the fuck are you destroying the walls?" Vinny asks me.

"Mind your own business," I tell him.

My brother looks around the room before his glare lands on me again. "Where's Kathryn?"

"She went home to her mother's place."

"You two have a fight?"

"No. Her mom needed help."

"So why do you look like someone pissed in your cereal?"

"Fuck off, Vinny," I yell at him, before bending down to swipe up my phone and check it.

The screen is cracked but it still works. So I dial her number again. And it goes right to voicemail *again*. Fuck it. I'll go to her mother's house. It's only a forty-five minute drive from here. I pick up my keys from my dresser and make my way out my bedroom door.

Vinny follows me down the stairs and into the garage. "What the fuck are you doing?" I ask him.

"Not letting you go anywhere by yourself when

you're clearly worked up." He jumps in the passenger seat of my car.

"Suit yourself." I shrug, sliding behind the wheel before punching Kathryn's mother's address into the GPS and driving out onto the street.

"Where we going?" Vinny asks a few minutes later.

I glare at him. "Kathryn's mother's house."

"Why?"

"Because her phone is switched off and she said she'd call me," I tell him.

"Fuck, I knew you had it bad but, Gray, this is insane. You're going to turn up at your girlfriend's mother's house after midnight because your girl didn't call you?" he asks.

"You don't know her. She wouldn't *not* call. Something is wrong."

"Okay." Vinny is quiet for the rest of the drive.

When I get to her mother's house, every light in the place is off. Maybe my brother is right. She probably just fell asleep. I should go home and wait until morning.

Fuck it. It's not like Kathryn's family is ever going to love me anyway. I'm a fucking Monroe. No mother in their right mind would want their daughter dating me.

"Wait here," I tell Vinny as I get out of the car.

I walk up to the front door and press the door-bell. There's nothing. Silence. The lights don't even switch on. I press it again. This time, I see a lamp illuminate a far window.

"Who is it?" an elderly woman's voice calls out through the door.

"It's Grayson Monroe, ma'am. I'm a friend of Kathryn's," I tell her.

"You're a friend of my daughter's?" the woman asks, cracking the door enough to eye me through the small opening.

I nod my head. "Yes, ma'am. Do you mind if I speak to her for a minute?"

Her eyebrows scrunch up. "Kathryn isn't here. I haven't seen or heard from my daughter in over two years. How do you know her?"

"That can't be right." I take my phone out of my pocket and pull up a photo of me and Kathryn. "This is her, right?"

The woman brings a hand to her mouth. "Yes, that's her. Where is she?"

"I don't know. I thought she'd be here. With you." A chill runs down my spine, and I can feel a wave of adrenaline course through my veins. I don't like where this is going.

"Please, if you see her, tell her to come home. Or just call me," the woman pleads.

"You really haven't seen her in two years?" I ask.

"No."

"I'm sorry to wake you," I say and walk back to the car, my mind whirling with each step I take.

Where the fuck are you, Kathryn?

I dial Liliana's number. "Hello?"

"Where is she, Liliana?" I growl into the phone.

"Who is this?"

"Grayson. Don't pretend you don't know who it is. Where the fuck is Kathryn?" I repeat.

"Why? What happened? Last time I heard from her, she was going to her mom's place," she says.

"When? When did you hear from her?"

"Around lunchtime. Why? What's going on?" Liliana asks.

"I gotta go. If you hear from her again, call me. And, Liliana, if I find out you're lying to me, if you know where she is... I don't give a fuck what your family's last name might be." I disconnect the call, not caring in the slightest that I've just threatened the Valentino princess.

My father might rule the underground here in Canada. But Liliana's family? They're old school Italian mafia, running things out of New York and over in Italy. In any other situation, I'd warn someone against doing what I just did. But right now, finding Kathryn is my priority. Fuck the consequences.

My stomach twists. What if someone took her? What if this is a direct attack on my family and they're using her against me? I've been such a fucking idiot. I haven't hidden how much that girl means to me. Anyone with eyes can tell she's my fucking world.

But then her mother's words come crashing back down on my shoulders. She said she hasn't seen her daughter in two years. Kathryn told me she's been going home to her mother's place during every last one of our school breaks.

Where was she really going if not there? Better yet, why would she lie to me about it?

Something isn't adding up. I'm missing something. Knowing it's useless, I press her number on my phone again. And again, it goes straight to her voicemail. "Kathryn, I don't care what's happening. Please call me back." I don't know how many messages I've left at this point.

"What happened?" Vinny asks when I get back in the car.

"She's not there," I tell him.

"Where is she?"

"No fucking idea." I turn on the ignition, and Vinny looks at me. I watch him through my peripheral vision. He's worried. And he should be. The whole fucking world should be if I don't find my girlfriend.

Chapter Six

Present

I park the car in the garage, letting the door close all the way before I get out. I knew coming back here wasn't a good idea. I thought enough time had passed. I'd hoped enough time had passed anyway.

Maybe it has. Maybe it hasn't. Still, I shouldn't be taking risks. But what was I supposed to do? I got word that my mom was dying. I came back for her. It killed me to stay away for so long. I mean, I have no one to blame but myself for the situation I'm in. The situation I put everyone else in with me, because of my actions.

I open the back door, and Graycee is already out of her seat belt and jumping up and down with an energy I only wish I could match. "Mama, I'm gonna put this on the special shelf. I'm never going to lose it," she says, holding up the puck that the Vancouver Knight's latest recruit gave her today at the junior league hockey practice.

When Graycee begged me to let her play hockey, I couldn't say no. I remember how much I'd wanted to play the game as a little girl, only to be forced into figure skating because, in my father's words, "Hockey isn't a girl sport."

My refusal to let my daughter grow up with limitations put on her because of her gender might have just blown my carefully laid cover. But she didn't recognize me. Aliyah Monroe, Gray's little sister, was right in front of me, and she had no signs of recognition.

Hopefully this will all go away on its own. I can try to find Graycee a new hockey team, one that won't have random Knights players dropping in to help coach for the day. We've been going to that rink for two months now, and not once have I heard mention of the NHL team or its association with the junior league. I did my research before registering Graycee. I couldn't find a link. I would never have let her join up if there were.

It's too close for comfort. He could find us. Not that he'd still be looking for me. I'm sure, by now, I'm nothing but a distant memory in Gray's mind. It's been six years. He's had six years to move on.

But he hasn't moved on, or at least not from what I read in the tabloids. He's not without female company, that much is evident. But as far as long-term relationships go, I haven't seen anything like that. And I've been looking. A lot. What can I say? I like to punish myself. Remind myself of the choices I made that landed me here.

"Mama, are you listening?" Graycee asks.

"What? Yes, baby. Go put it on your good shelf." I smile down at my daughter and step aside so she can climb out of the car.

"Mr. King was so nice. Can we go see him, Mama?"

"No, Graycee, we can't just go and see him. Liam King is a busy man," I tell her.

"Can we watch the game?" she asks.

"What game?"

"The Knights game. Why don't we watch Knights games?"

As much as we love watching hockey together, the Vancouver Knights are the one team we don't follow. Well, I don't let Graycee follow anyway. I knew she was going to find out about them eventually. It's unavoidable with how well they've been doing in the league. I was just hoping to keep it from her for as long as I could.

"Um, I don't know. They're just not a good team, baby," I say. It's not the truth, the Knights are one of the best. Especially now. I usually watch the replays when Graycee is asleep. And every time I see Gray's face on the screen, it's like a knife stabbing right through my heart.

"Well, I think they are. Mr. King was so good," Graycee says.

"He was. Come on, go put that away. We're going to get changed really quick and then go see Nana," I tell her.

"At the hospital again?"

"Yes, Graycee, at the hospital."

"I don't like it there," she says.

"I don't either, but Nana needs our company."

Graycee runs off down the hall, and I pull out my phone. I've been avoiding making this call. I don't even know if she still has the same number, and I really don't know how she's going to respond to me after our last encounter...

"Please don't do this, Kathryn. I'm begging you. I can fix this. I can go to my dad and he'll help. Whatever you're running from, it can't be scarier than him, right?" Liliana pleads with me.

The tears fall down my face. "I'm sorry. I can't. I can't do this to him. Please, just when he asks— because he will—tell him the last you heard, I was going to my mother's."

"I don't like it. He's been so good to you, Kathryn. Tell me what happened? Did he do something? Did someone else do something?"

"No, it's not him. It's me. I did something, and now the only way I can help him is to disappear. I have to."

I shake off the memory and dial the number I've had memorized for the past six years.

"Hello?" a familiar voice answers, and it's all I can do to not burst into tears.

"Liliana...?"

I hear her gasp on the other end of the line. "Kathryn? Is that you?" she asks. When I don't say anything, she sighs. "Kathryn?"

"It's me," I tell her.

"Oh my god! Thank you, Baby Jesus. Where are you? Are you okay? I can have the jet ready in thirty minutes. Tell me where you are and I'll come to you." She's speaking so fast I don't know how to respond.

I walk into my bathroom and turn on the tap, and that's when I let the tears mix with the sound of running water. I don't want Graycee to see me upset. It will only worry her. I remember when she found me crying after watching one of Gray's games once. She wiped my cheeks with her little hands and started crying with me. And it broke my heart all over again.

"I'm so sorry," I say. "I didn't know who else to call."

"It's okay. What's happening? How have you been? *Where* have you been?" Liliana asks.

"I've been okay. I'm back. In Vancouver," I tell her.

"Oh," she says. "*Oh!*" she repeats with more emphasis. "Does he know?"

"No. I can't let him know, Lil. I ran into his little sister today, and I don't know... I guess it freaked me out."

"You saw Aliyah? Did she recognize you?"

"I don't think so. She didn't say anything. She was with Liam King," I say.

"Well, yeah, now I get it. It's easy to not notice anything or anyone else in the room with that man hanging around." Liliana laughs.

"What if she remembers and tells him I'm back?"

"What's the worst that could happen if he found out?" she counters.

"He could take her away from me," I say. "They could find me. They could hurt her."

"Take who? And who's *they*?" Liliana presses for answers I can't give her.

"I'm sorry. I shouldn't have done this. I'm so sorry, Lil. Forget I called." I hang up the phone, feeling worse than I did a few minutes ago.

What the hell was I thinking? I can't get her involved in my mess again.

Graycee is asleep in the chair by my mother's hospital bed. I look at her perfect little expression. I watch my daughter sleep a lot. She has my heart-shaped face, small button nose, and blonde hair—although no one would know that right now, seeing as I'm currently a redhead. She has her father's big, pouty lips and green eyes though.

My heart breaks for her, that she'll never know how amazing he is. How much I'm sure he would have loved her. I took that from her. I'm not delusional. I know it's my fault that she doesn't have it. But sometimes sacrifices have to be made, and I chose to make one that I can't undo.

"Something happened today. You're quiet," my mom says.

The doctors claim she only has a few weeks left.

But they don't know my mom. She's a fighter. And I'm not ready to lose her.

"I saw his little sister," I admit.

My mom is well aware of the Grayson Monroe situation. I went to her first, all those years ago, and I had her lie to him. I had her tell him she didn't know me anymore. That she hadn't seen me for two years. It was the only way I could think of to get him to back off. It worked too. My mom said he never returned after the first night when he showed up on her doorstep looking for me.

"Did she recognize you?"

"I don't think so. But what if it clicks later, you know?"

"Do you really think he'd still be looking for you after all this time, Kathryn?" my mom asks.

I know she thinks I'm crazy, that there is no way a guy I dated in college would be that hung up on me that he'd keep looking six years later. And perhaps I am crazy, but I still ache. There is a part of me that hasn't stopped aching ever since I left. I don't think this gaping hole I created will ever fill back up.

"I don't know," I say.

"You have her. You see him every day because you have her. You're reminded of him. He doesn't have that, Kathryn."

"I know. You're right. Even if he did find out I was back in town, it's not like he's going to come looking for me." I'm driving myself insane for no reason. "But what if he does...? What if he takes her?"

Gray's family is powerful. They have a team of lawyers at their disposal at any given time. Then again, they're the freaking Canadian mafia. If they really wanted her, they'd just take her and there wouldn't be a damn thing I could do to get her back.

One thing I know for certain is I broke my own damn soul to save him. Which means I'll do far more than that to protect our daughter. I haven't gone through hell and back for everything to blow up in my face. No good can come from Gray finding me. No matter how much a part of me might want him to.

Chapter Seven

Grayson

I'm currently sitting around a table at a local club with the four Valentino brothers, their wives, and some of our players. Oh yeah, and my little sister, who is cozying up to one of my teammates. And all I want to do is reach over and strangle the fucking life out of King. Liam fucking King. The team's new hotshot player. Sure, the guy's a fucking asset on the ice. I was even starting to like him.

That was before I found out he was screwing my little sister.

I look at Aliyah. Dad's right. She looks happy. Content even. I haven't seen her look like this in, well, ever. She's been happy before I guess, but there's always been a dark cloud around her. My sister went through the kind of shit no little girl should ever go through.

Speaking of little girls...

My mind wanders to the screenshot of that newspaper clipping I still have on my phone. The one of the little girl and her mother. I've been staring at it for weeks, trying to figure out what the fuck to do about it. If I want to do something about it...

I have no idea.

"I'm going to dance," Aliyah announces before shooting up from her seat. She whispers something to King, and a look crosses his face that makes me want to put my damn fist through it.

"You know she'll get bored of you, right?" I tell him once my sister is out of earshot. I have no idea if that's true or not. It's probably wishful thinking on my part. But he doesn't need to know that. The cocksucker isn't good enough for my little sister.

"That's not possible. Unlike some of us, I'm not fucking boring." The asshole smiles at me.

"Well, damn, he's got you there, Gray." Matteo Valentino snickers. The fucker likes to think he's funny. Guess that comes with being the spare.

"Fuck off, Matteo." I pull my phone out of my pocket, load the picture of the newspaper clipping on my screen, and slide it across the table to King.

"Who is this?" I ask, pointing at the little girl in the photo.

"A kid from that youth league appearance your sister made me do," he says.

"What's her name?"

"Why? What do you want with her? She's just a fucking kid, Grayson," King snaps.

"What's her name?" I ask a little more forcefully this time around.

"I don't know. Graycee or something like that." He shrugs.

"Graycee." Her name rolls off my tongue. *Graycee*, I repeat the name in my head. Over and over again. Pointing back at the screen, I tap the woman in the photo. "And is that her mother? The woman behind her?"

"Yeah."

"Fuck!" I hiss out, nearly flipping the table when

I stand and storm my way through the crowded bar before exiting out the side door into the back alley. Where my fist then slams into the closest brick wall. "Fuck! Fuck! Fuck her!"

"Whoa. Monroe, what the fuck?" Luke, the team's top forward, takes hold of my wrist, spinning me around and shoving me against the wall.

"Fuck off, Luke," I snarl and shove him back.

"Yeah, you'll have to try harder than that, man. Who's the chick?" He juts his chin towards the phone still clutched in my hand.

Luke has been my best friend since the day we were both drafted straight out of college. I've told him everything. Everything but this. About her. I haven't even spoken her name aloud. I've thought about her, every fucking day. Not that I wanted to. It was like I'd wake up, search for her, and realize she's not there. Six. Fucking. Years. Later.

I've tried to fuck her out of my system. I've fucked so many puck bunnies, models, actresses that I've lost count. They're all just a blur of nameless faces and bodies. But her? She haunts my mind like a fucking obsession I just can't shake.

Every day, without fail, I looked for her. For two fucking years. I went as far as to hire a private investigator, turned over every fucking stone I could find, and nothing. She disappeared off the face of the earth. Vanished without a single fucking trace.

I've blamed myself. All this time, I thought if I just went with her that day... If I had been more insistent on driving her to her mother's house...

The worst-case scenarios of what could have happened to her played out like horror movies in my dreams. For years, I'd wake up in a cold sweat, screaming her name. Fucking Kathryn Kilgor. And now she's back. She's back and I don't know how I'm supposed to feel about any of it. I wanted to find her. I've never *not* wanted to find her. I just gave up on the notion of that ever happening. I mourned a woman who was gone but not dead. A woman who is very much alive and well. A woman who I'm going to fucking find and make pay for what she did to me. What she did to us.

"Who is she, Gray?" Luke asks again.

"She was supposed to be mine," is all I say as my knees collapse and my ass hits the ground.

Luke squats down in front of me. "What does that mean?"

I shake my head and look at the photo on my screen. I know it's her. I never had any doubt about that. She can change her hair color, but I know her.

Or at least I thought I did. Then my eyes flick to the little girl in front of her. Graycee.

"I don't want any babies if they're not yours, Gray. I want a little girl with your green eyes. We'll name her Graycee, and I already know she's going to be a huge daddy's girl."

Kathryn's words replay in my mind. We had plans. We had our whole future laid out. Marriage, kids, hockey. It was all supposed to be ours. Together.

And then she fucking left.

She left and took a piece of me with her. Graycee. I don't need a DNA test to tell me that child is mine. Tears spring to my eyes. I look up to my best friend.

"She was supposed to be mine," I repeat.

"Okay," he says. "Start at the beginning."

"We met in college. Kathryn. We dated for two years and then I brought her home for break. To meet the family. She disappeared. One day she was there. The next she wasn't," I tell him.

"She ran?"

"I don't know. I thought... All these years, I thought she was dead. I thought I brought her into my world and someone had taken her." I stare down at the photo. "But she's not dead. She chose to leave.

74

Why would she do that to me?" I ask while knowing full well that Luke doesn't have any of those answers.

"I don't know, man." He runs a hand through his hair. "What are we doing about this?"

The thing about Luke is nothing is ever just him or me. It's always *us*. He's got my back, no matter the situation. This is different, though. I don't think he can help me this time.

"I need to go find her," I say.

"And when you do? What'll you do?"

Wrap my hands around her pretty little fucking neck and watch the life drain from her eyes. I don't say it out loud, but Luke can see it clear as day on my face.

"No." He shakes his head. "You're not doing anything about this tonight. You're going to sleep on it. We are so fucking close, Gray. This is our year for the Cup. I'm not letting you spiral." He pushes to his feet. "Come on, let's go home." Then he holds out a hand to me.

I take it and pull myself up off the ground. "She's supposed to be mine," I say again.

"Sleep on it. For a few days. Right now, you're in no frame of mind to confront her. You need to get control of yourself, Gray," Luke says.

I follow him down the alleyway, over to where

his car is parked behind the building. I'm numb as I open the door and slide into the passenger seat. The urge to go and find her, ask why she did this to us, why she stole not only herself from me, but our child... *That* urge is fucking strong.

"She's mine," I hiss under my breath.

"So you've said," Luke replies.

"Not Kathryn, the kid. The little girl in this photo. She's mine," I tell him.

"Are you sure? That's a big deal, Gray."

Finally he fucking gets it!

"I'm a hundred percent certain," I say, looking at the photo for the millionth time. The same shade of green eyes stare back at me.

"DNA test, bro. That's all I'm saying about that. You are in a position that many women are looking to take advantage of. Don't do anything without concrete evidence."

"I don't need a test. She's mine."

"I think what you need is to sleep on it," he repeats. "Get in the right mindset. If it's true, and that little girl is yours, then we will do something about it. But first, sleep. Then we're going to come up with a plan to find out the truth. What we're not going to do is act on emotion and go off the deep end."

I ignore him. I don't give a fuck what anyone says. I'm going to find Kathryn, and when I do, she's going to answer for what she did. I've been in love with this woman for so fucking long. I never believed for one minute that she would have left voluntarily. I knew Kathryn, and the girl I knew wouldn't have done that to me.

Except she fucking did.

I'm fuming. My blood is boiling. It's that same feeling I get out on the ice whenever I see someone make a dirty play against one of my guys. It's why I'm the team's fucking enforcer. It's in my blood, the violence, the vengeance.

And right now, that fiery rage is all directed at her. The one person I never thought I'd be capable of hurting. I'm imagining the fear in her eyes while I strangle the life out of her. I'm imagining watching her lifeless body fall to the fucking floor. And then I see that little girl's face.

"Fuck!" I jump out of the car as soon as Luke pulls into the driveway. I can't just fucking sit here and do nothing. That's not me. I head for the garage and rush inside my Lambo. The engine purrs to life and then I'm flying back onto the street. Right past Luke, who is yelling God knows what at me.

A few minutes later, I'm stopping outside her

mother's house. I know she lives here. I've kept tabs on the old woman, in case Kathryn ever did come back. Given I haven't checked in on her in the last six months, but I'm still pretty sure she owns the place.

I get out of my car and walk down the darkened street, pausing in front of the house. Kathryn is in the living room. I can see her. Sitting there. On the sofa. Reading a book. The curtains are wide open and the lights are on. If she's trying to hide, she's doing a shitty fucking job at it.

As if she can sense me, she looks up and right at the window. I know she can't see me from where I'm presently standing in the shadows. I'm about to step out, cross the road, and walk right up to the door when the little girl walks into the room. Kathryn's eyes widen. She gets up from the chair and pulls the girl into her arms before walking over and shutting the curtain. She's too far away for me to see the fear in her eyes, but she's scared. I can tell. It's obvious in the way she moves.

The question is who has her so on edge? Is it me? Or someone else?

Chapter Eight

Kathryn

I'm driving myself mad. I keep thinking he's here. Like he's just standing out there, somewhere, watching me. He's not. I know that, but that feeling I only ever got when he was around, that sense of safety that only Gray could give me... I've had that for a few brief moments.

And then, like a match burning out, it's gone and replaced by an overwhelming sense of fear. I asked the doctors if I could move my mother to another town; even just the next town over would be preferable to staying here. They told me there was nothing they could do to arrange the transport and it'd be detrimental to her health to move her.

"Graycee, you almost ready, baby?" I call out. Mornings are not her favorite, and getting ready for school isn't high on her priority list. She doesn't answer. "Graycee?" I try again while packing a sandwich into her lunchbox. When she still doesn't respond, I drop everything and run down the hall. "Graycee?"

"What?" she finally calls back when I stop in the doorway of her bedroom.

"You didn't answer me. You almost ready?" I ask her.

"Uh-huh," she says. She's standing in front of the full-length mirror, staring at her reflection.

"What are you looking at?" I ask before walking into her room.

"Do I look like him?"

"Who?"

"My daddy? At school, everyone is drawing pictures of their parents. I drew you, but it's just you,

Mama. I thought I could just draw a daddy in, but I don't know what he looks like," she says.

I'm speechless. It's not the first time Graycee has asked about her father. And I've always answered her questions about him, right down to telling her that his name is Grayson. When she asked why he didn't live with us, that was a hard one to answer. I dodged it without giving her anything concrete. I was sick that whole night, throwing up at the thought of what I'd done to both of them.

I turn her around to face me. "You have his eyes. Your daddy has the most amazing green eyes, Graycee, just like yours. And you have his lips," I say, brushing her hair off her face.

"Okay. I'll draw a man with green eyes then," she tells me with a nod.

I smile, but don't say anything more. What can I say? It's just a class drawing. It's not like she's asking to go find him.

I walk Graycee into her class, glancing over my shoulder before exiting the school. Someone is watching me. I can feel it. But whenever I look, I can't find anyone or anything out of the ordinary. So I shake the feeling off.

When I get back to my car, I lock the door and drive home. I park in the garage and wait for the door to close before I get out. I can't shake the sense that he's here. I really am going freaking mad, because when I walk through the kitchen and into Graycee's room to tidy it up, I swear I can smell him.

I plug in my headphones and turn on some music. I need to figure out how to get over this stupid feeling. Ever since I saw Aliyah, I've been off. That's a lie. I've been off ever since we came back to Vancouver.

I go about my morning routine of cleaning, even

going as far as to scrub the bathroom and kitchen. I look at the clock on the living room wall when there's a knock at the door. It's eleven a.m. I freeze. Whoever it is will go away. No one knows I'm here. I don't have any friends who just drop in.

But the knocking continues. "Kathryn, open up. I know you're in there," a familiar voice yells out.

I gasp and run to the door, swinging it open, and am met by Liliana. She's not alone though. There's a huge guy behind her. A huge guy I know. Well, a guy I *know of*, from watching TSN. Travis O'Neil, a New York hockey player.

I don't have time to say anything before Liliana practically jumps on me, throwing her arms around my neck. "I knew you'd be here!" she squeals.

"What? What are you doing here?" I ask while peering over her shoulder to look at the street behind her. It's empty.

"Looking for you," she says, finally releasing me. "Are you okay? No, of course you're not. You wouldn't have called if you were." She's talking so fast it's hard to keep up.

"Come in." I step out of the doorway to give her room to enter.

"Oh, this is Travis." Lil waves a hand over to the hulking man blindly following behind her.

"I know who he is, Lil." I chuckle.

"Right, Kathryn's a big hockey fan," she tells Travis.

"It's nice to meet you," he says politely.

"Yeah, um, you too," I reply and then look back at Lil. "I can't believe you're here." I choke up.

"Travis, can you go down to that Starbucks we passed on the way over and grab us a couple of coffees?" Lil asks.

He looks from me to her. "I'd rather stay."

"Too bad. You can't. I'm fine. Go. Give me ten minutes to talk to my friend who I haven't seen in six years," she tells him.

"Fine," he grunts and walks back out the door.

Lil spins on me. "Now, tell me *everything*."

I burst into tears. "I missed you so much!"

"I know. Me too. But we can talk about that later. What's going on?" she urges me again.

"I didn't want to leave. I didn't have a choice. But I did leave and I need to stay gone. He can't find me, Lil."

"Who? Gray?" she asks.

I nod my head.

"Why are you so afraid of him? I get that he can be questionable at times, but I've known the guy for a while now, Kathryn, and I can't see him hurting a woman, especially you. Not that I wouldn't believe you if you were to tell me otherwise," she says.

"No, he wouldn't. He didn't," I say. I'm not too sure about now, though. I have no idea what he'd do if he found me, if he found out about Graycee... I don't think he'd hurt me physically, but there are other ways someone can hurt a person. I should know. I hurt us both.

"Okay, on the phone, you said you were worried he'd take her?" Lil asks while her eyes flick around the living room. She spots the photos I've hung up of Graycee. "Oh, Kathryn." She gasps before walking over and picking up a frame that's sitting on a shelf at eye level. "Please tell me this is a long-lost niece or cousin or something."

I shake my head. "That's Graycee, my daughter."

"Graycee," she says. "First, she's beautiful. Second, what the fuck were you thinking?" Her voice hardens.

"I didn't have a choice," I tell her.

"Everyone has choices, Kathryn. The one you made, though? It was the wrong one."

"It wasn't," I insist. "I did what I had to do."

Liliana looks at me. She collapses onto the sofa and shakes her head. "You know, I think he'd forgive you for just about anything. He loves you that much, but this? Taking his kid, Kathryn? I don't know if that's something even Gray will forgive you for."

"I'm not looking for his forgiveness, because he's not going to find me," I remind her. "It's been six years, Lil. He's not still looking for me."

"March eighteenth. Every year, he mourns you like you died, Kathryn. You know how I know that? Because I've flown out here on that day, every year, to help him through it. Do you have any idea what it's been like watching him fall apart? He looked for you for years, Kathryn. And even though I knew it was your choice, I always hoped he'd find you and bring you back."

"I'm sorry. I'm sorry." I'm sobbing now. "I didn't know I was pregnant when I left. I really didn't know. I can't... He can't find me, Lil."

"What are you running from, Kathryn? Because it sure as hell isn't Grayson Monroe."

"I... I did something. I shouldn't have done it. It was stupid. Reckless. But I did it, and I got caught," I tell her. "I don't want you to get involved. It's not safe, Lil."

Liliana laughs. "Are you serious right now? You do know who my family is, right?"

"I know. But I can't be the reason someone targets you."

"How can I help?" she asks with a long sigh. "If you need to disappear, I'll help you because you're my best friend, Kathryn. But please, please don't ask me to do that again."

"I can't leave yet. My mom... she doesn't have much time left. I need to be with her while we can."

"Where is Graycee now?"

"At school. I have to go pick her up soon."

"Okay." Liliana nods her head. "I want to meet her. Can I meet her?"

"She doesn't know about me, Lil. She doesn't know that I ran away with her..."

"It's okay. I won't say anything," Lil assures me. Then there's a knock at the door and I jump. "It's just Travis." She gets up to let him in, and Travis steps inside the living room with two Starbucks cups; he hands them to Liliana before offering me another polite nod.

Chapter Nine

Grayson

I've been watching her for weeks. Waiting for the perfect moment to let her know I've found her. I don't know why I haven't just jumped out of the shadows yet. There's something about watching her with Graycee that keeps me rooted to the spot.

Kathryn loves that little girl. I can see that. She's a good mother, but I always knew she would be. Then again, would a good mother deny their child a father? I don't know. I didn't exactly have the best role models growing up.

Fuck, my father killed my mother when he discovered what she'd been doing to my little sister. It wasn't until Mom had sliced right down Aliyah's wrists in her attempt to kill her own daughter that Dad found out. It wasn't even a question. He killed her on the spot. At the time, I didn't understand how a husband could kill his wife. But I get it now. He chose his child. Which was the right fucking thing to do.

I put cameras all throughout Kathryn's mother's house. Watching her on this tiny screen has become my new obsession. I know I need to stop. I need to do something about this so I can get back to focusing on the game. We're so close to winning it all. I can feel it. There are only a couple more rounds in the play-offs before I'm holding that Cup up over my head.

She was supposed to be there for that moment. She could be, if I go and get her now. The problem is, when I do make my move, I'm not going to let her go. Not because I still want her. I don't. How could I want someone who's done what she's done to me?

Just because I don't want her doesn't mean I want anyone else to have her either.

"Grayson, my office now." My father's voice booms through the locker room.

I look up from my phone. And then down at myself. I'm not even out of my gear yet. "Sure, give me a minute," I tell him.

Dad nods his head and walks out. Luke and King are both staring at me. "What?" I bark at them.

"You waiting for an invitation, Cap?" Luke asks with a raised brow.

I glance around the locker room. The rest of the guys are in various stages of showering and dressing. Getting ready to leave. Meanwhile, I came in off the ice, picked up my phone, and started watching Kathryn and Graycee like the fucking stalker I am. I haven't moved since.

"Why? You offering?"

"In your dreams." Luke laughs while running a hand over his torso.

I screw up my face, drop my phone to the bench, and bend over to untie my skates.

"You good?" King asks.

"Why?" I might have to play nice with the guy on the ice, but we're not *on the ice* right now.

"Aliyah is worried about you," he says.

I glare at him. Hearing my sister's name come out of his mouth makes me want to jam my fist into his skull again. Everyone on the team knows my dislike for the fucker. I mean, he's fucking dating my little sister. Of course I hate the prick.

"My sister isn't any of your concern," I tell him.

"Oh my god, Gray, grow up already." Speak of the devil and she shall appear. Aliyah's heels tap on the tiled floor as she makes her way across the locker room over to where we're sitting.

"Fucking cover yourselves up," I growl at my teammates.

King walks up to my sister and stands in front of her, blocking her view of the entire room. I smirk. *Yeah, that's not going to stop her.* And, sure enough, Aliyah steps right around him.

She sits down next to me, not caring that she's in a locker room full of half-naked NHL players. "We need to talk," she says.

"What about?" I ask, my eyes refocused on my laces.

"You," she says. "You're distracted. What's going on? Is it Kathryn? Have you seen her yet?"

"Aliyah, this isn't something you need to worry yourself about," I tell her, finally getting one skate off and starting on the other.

"You are something I worry about, whether you like it or not. So talk. How can I help?" she asks.

"You can help by getting me a coaching gig in that junior league."

"She's yours, isn't she? That little girl?" Aliyah shakes her head. "I should have noticed. I should have seen it."

"How could you know?" I ask her. "It seems I've had a fucking kid out in the world for almost six years and *I* didn't even know it."

"How certain are you? I feel like a DNA test is necessary, Gray. She left. Maybe she was..."

"Do not finish that fucking thought, Lia," I grunt before pushing to my feet. "I gotta go see Dad, and you need to get the fuck out of this locker room."

"Don't worry, Gray, there's only one naked body in here I'm interested in looking at." Aliyah smiles as her gaze scans over to King, who is leaning against his locker staring right at us.

"You deserve better," I tell her.

"We've had this discussion. More than once, Gray. I happen to like him. A lot. So you need to accept it." She moves to stand toe to toe with me. "Come on, let's go see what Dad wants with you. I bet it's to chew your ass out for that performance during practice. Or lack thereof," she mutters under her breath.

"You giving up the PR thing and moving into coaching, Lia?" I laugh.

Her arm snaps out to whack me across the stomach. I don't feel a thing. I've still got all my gear on, sans the skates.

"I'll line up a gig at the junior league for you," she says. "But you need to promise me to stop hating on my boyfriend."

I look at her with a raised brow, before wrapping an arm around her shoulder and leading her out of the locker room. "Lia, you're my baby sister. I'm never going to stop hating on your boyfriend. Ever," I tell her.

I knock on my father's office door, then open it

and walk in. "You wanted to see me?" I announce my presence, observing that he isn't alone. My Uncle Lou is with him.

"Come, sit down," Dad says before his eyes land on my sister. "Aliyah, I'm sure you've got more pressing things to be doing than escorting your brother around the arena."

"Mmm, not really. But I can tell when a girl's not wanted." She turns on her heels and walks right back out of the room.

"What the fuck is going on with you?" Dad says, cutting right to the chase.

"Nothing." I sit back in the chair and fold my arms over my chest.

"Nothing? You're slacking. You're distracted, and you're moping around like someone ran over your dog."

I don't say a word. What the fuck am I supposed to say?

My college girlfriend, who I thought was dead, has suddenly resurfaced. Resurrected? And, oh, she's not alone. No, it seems I have a kid we didn't know about. Congratulations, you're a grandfather?

Yeah, I don't think so.

"Whatever it is, we can't help you if you don't tell us, Grayson," Uncle Lou says.

"I don't need help." Especially not the kind of help he'd be willing to give me. My uncle shoots first and asks questions later. Literally. "I'll fix my game," I tell them both. "Are we done here?"

My father looks at me, silently assessing my face, my body language, before nodding his head. I take that answer, jump up, and walk right out of there. I'm not an idiot, though. I know this conversation isn't over. And he's right. My game has been suffering. It fucking happened when she first disappeared too. I played like shit the rest of that year. I never got that C after Westin left back then. I was too distracted. Stuck in my own fucking head.

I need to fix this. Now.

I stomp back to the locker room, not surprised to find Luke waiting for me. "What your old man want?" he asks.

"To tell me my game sucked," I grunt while ripping my jersey over my head. Followed by my pads. I pick up my towel and stalk over to the showers. Luke follows behind me.

"I know I said that you should wait until after the playoffs, but maybe you should go and talk to her. Get it done, out of your head?" he says.

"Yeah, maybe," I tell him.

After rinsing off, I get dressed, pack my bag, and

walk out to my truck. I look at my phone and check the cameras. Kathryn isn't home. I know she's been spending a lot of time at the hospital with her mother. I should wait until Graycee is at school to make my move. I don't want to scare the little girl. And honestly, right now, I'm not sure what I'm going to do when I confront my ex.

I drive home and head straight for the games room, which is usually filled with a shit-ton of my friends. But I've told them not to come around the last few weeks. My house has always been the hangout spot. Expecting to find the room empty, I stop short when I see my siblings, with King all hung up on my sister again.

"What the fuck are you all doing here?" I ask. "And why the fuck aren't you at school?" I point to Jonah. The kid is in a graduate program. He's getting his MBA. He should not be here in Vancouver.

"We're here to help you. Stop with the growly thing and just sit down," Aliyah snaps.

My sister might be little but, fuck, she's got a nasty bite. There's also the whole *not being able to say no to her* thing I have going on. I've never been able to deny her anything. I'm not sure if it's because I've been overcompensating, trying to make up for what our mother did to her. Or if it's more me wanting to wrap her up and protect her—once again, because of our mother.

"We know about Kathryn being back," Jonah says, then adds, "I'm sorry."

"Why are you sorry? Kathryn being back in town is nothing. It doesn't mean anything. She left. Now she's back. Not a big deal." I shrug and walk up to the bar. I can't deal with this shit sober.

"What about the kid? That mean something?" Vinny asks.

I glare at him. "Leave it alone."

Vinny is a younger version of my father. Our old man is grooming him to take over the family businesses—the underground side of things anyway.

He raises his hands. "Give me some credit, Gray. I wouldn't hurt a fucking kid. Kathryn, though? After what she did to you, I'd be more than happy to take her out. And I would, if I didn't think you'd put a bullet through my head for doing so," he says.

As much as I fucking hate Kathryn right now, I don't want her dead. I've spent six years mourning her. I can't fucking do that shit again. "Don't touch her, Vinny. I mean it." I pour a glass full of Scotch, pick it up, and then set it back down.

Fuck this. I need to get out of here.

Chapter Ten

I pick Graycee up out of the car. She fell asleep as soon as we left the hospital. I think the long days are taking a toll on her. School, followed by the rink for an hour or so most days, and then we're at the hospital.

I don't know what else to do, though. If I don't

take her up to see my mom, she's not going to know her. I've kept her away for so long. I can see the heartache in my mom's eyes whenever she looks at her granddaughter.

We limited ourselves to one holiday a year over the last five years, since Graycee was born. I didn't trust that people weren't watching my mother's movements. It was always hard saying goodbye to her. I know that it's my own fault, but that doesn't mean it still doesn't cut me to the core.

Graycee is the one who's missed out. She's never had a family, other than me. She doesn't know what it's like to be surrounded by a whole team of people who love you. She would have had that with the Monroes. I have no doubt that they would have loved her.

After tucking my daughter into her bed, I kiss her forehead. "I'm so sorry, baby girl," I whisper before walking out of the room.

I go back to the front of the house and check the locks. I look out the window, and that feeling hits me again. That sensation that he's here. I know he's not. We've been staying at my mother's place for months. I ran into his sister weeks ago. If he knew I was in town, he would have shown up by now.

Unless he doesn't care anymore, which I

wouldn't blame him for. But I know Gray, and I know our love. It's not the kind you can just turn off. At least it's not for me. I always thought it was the same for him too. People do grow, though. Change as we get older and wiser and all that bullshit.

My mom could be right. Maybe I'm still hung up on him because I'm the one who left. I've had Graycee the whole time, a piece of him with me, while all he's had is a memory. By now, I'm sure I'm nothing more than a distant one at that.

I walk into my bedroom. I don't bother with the lights. I'm just as exhausted as Graycee is. All I want to do is lie down and sleep. I make it three steps over the threshold when the bedside lamp turns on.

I freeze.

"Kathryn, it's been a while." His voice... it's deeper than I remember. Raspier. Cold even.

A shiver runs through me. And not the kind that he used to elicit from my body. No, this one is nothing but pure dread. I look over my shoulder. Graycee's room is right across the hall. I can see her sleeping on her bed from here, her nightlight casting just enough illumination that I can make out her little body.

"Close the door," Gray says.

I turn back to him and my arm reaches out to

close the door before I stop myself. "No. What are you doing here?"

Grayson Monroe is sitting on my bed, his back resting against the headboard. "Close the door, Kathryn," he says again.

"I can't," I tell him. Gray tilts his head. He doesn't say anything, just stares at me. "What are you doing here?"

"Two thousand, one hundred, and eighty-four days," he says. "That's how long I've been looking for you. So, imagine my surprise when you show up right here, in Vancouver, on my metaphorical doorstep, after all this time."

"You need to leave. You can't be here."

Gray throws his legs over the side of the bed and walks over to me, his steps measured. Assured. His six-foot-two frame towering over me. I take a step backwards. I was never afraid of Grayson. I knew what he was capable of doing to people. But I never feared him. Until right now.

My back hits the wall. Gray's hands land on each side of my head, his face leaning into me. "You lost the right to tell me what the fuck to do six years ago, Kathryn," he growls.

I swallow the lump in my throat. My head turns to the side. I can't let Graycee see this. I need to get him out of here. "You need to leave," I repeat. My hands land on his chest, attempting to push him away from me.

That was my first mistake. Touching him. My hands freeze and my entire body goes into some kind of shock. I shouldn't have touched him. It's not like I can push him off me anyway. Gray steps closer to me. His thigh presses between my legs while one of his hands wraps around my neck. Memories of how much I loved when he used to do this flash through my mind. I force myself to not look away. To meet his angry glare head-on.

"Fuck you," he snarls in a low tone. "Fuck you," he says it again and again as his hand squeezes tighter.

I grab at his wrists, trying to loosen the grip he has on me. "Gray, stop. You're hurting me," I rasp out.

He chuckles, but it sounds more sinister than an actual laugh. "Hurting you? Oh, babe, I haven't even started that part yet."

My blood goes cold. This isn't the Gray I knew. Gone is the easygoing, carefree guy I used to love. And standing in front of me is someone else entirely.

"Mama?" My daughter's voice has my eyes

widening. Gray immediately drops his hand and takes a step back.

"Graycee, baby, go back to bed," I tell her, not taking my focus off Gray, who is staring at my daughter.

"Who are you?" Graycee asks. "Why are you hurting my mama?"

I choke on a sob. "Mama is okay. But I need you to go back to bed," I tell her. I'm desperate to get her out of the room. Gray steps towards where Graycee is still standing in the doorway. "Gray, no." I try to step around him but then he drops to his knees in front of her, before holding out a hand.

"Hi, Graycee. I'm Grayson," he introduces himself.

Graycee's eyes widen, matching my own shock, and she peers up at me before looking back at him. "You're my daddy?"

The room is silent, except for the rapid beat of my heart pounding in my head.

"Yeah, I am," Gray says.

"Are you finished being busy? Are you going to live with me now?" Graycee asks him.

"Come on, baby, let's go back to bed." I step around Gray and pick up my daughter.

"As a matter of fact, I *am* going to live with you

now, Graycee. Would you like that?" Gray pushes to his feet, meeting my daughter's eyes. *Our* daughter's eyes.

She nods her head. "I've been waiting."

My heart breaks for her, and when I look at the pain evident on Gray's face, it breaks for them both.

"Why don't you go to your room and pick the things you want to bring with you the most?" Gray says.

I glare at him. What the hell is he talking about?

He reaches out to Graycee. And she, of course, jumps into his arms—none the wiser that I want nothing more than to hold her tighter so she can't. "Come on, I'll help you. Mama needs to grab her own bag," Gray adds while looking straight at me.

"Where are we going?" Graycee asks him.

"Home," he says. "I'm taking you home, Graycee."

"And Mama?"

"Yes, and Mama too." He turns to me. "Pack a bag, Kathryn. We're leaving in five minutes with or without you," he whispers that last part into my ear as he walks right past me and into Graycee's room.

I stare after him. He's not going to hurt her. I know that. Me, on the other hand? I'm not too sure. My mind is telling me to do something. To go and grab my daughter and run again. I can't lose her. But my legs won't move. My knees buckle, and I grab on to the doorframe to stop myself from falling.

"Can I bring my gear? And my puck! I need my puck. It's really special," Graycee prattles on, wide awake and full of excitement now. She's so trusting, just falls right into his arms.

Then again, she has no reason not to be. I've only ever told her the truth about her father. That he's a kind, good man. That he would do anything for her if she needed him to. Because that's the Grayson I once knew. I just hope to God that version of him is still in there somewhere.

"Where's this special puck?" Gray asks her.

"On my shelf, here." Graycee runs over to grab it. "Mr. Liam King gave it to me. He's the best hockey player in all the world," she says with a huge smile on her face. "Do you like hockey?"

"I love hockey," Gray tells her.

"Maybe you can take us to Mr. King's game. I asked Mama and she said she'd think about it."

"I can take you to as many hockey games as you want, Graycee." Gray looks down at the tiny bag she packed. "Is that all you want to take?"

"Yep." She nods. "Where is home? Do you have a dog?"

"Ah, no, I don't have a dog. And home isn't far from here," he says while taking her hockey bag from her arms. Graycee is still clutching her puck, and Gray stares at it like he wants to tear it out of her little hands. And maybe burn it.

"Mama, are you okay?" Graycee asks when she turns to me.

Gray looks from my daughter to me with concern on his face. "You get your stuff?"

I shake my head. "I'm okay, Graycee. Why don't you go to the bathroom, and don't forget to wash your hands," I remind her.

"Can you hold this? But don't drop it. It's special. It has Mr. King's autograph." Graycee hands Gray her prized puck.

"Got it. Won't drop it. Promise," he tells her.

I wait until she closes the bathroom door before glaring at him. "What are you doing?"

"Taking my daughter home. Where she should have fucking been for the last five years," he growls. "Six. 'Cause I would have loved the fucking chance to be there before she was born too."

"You can't take her from me," I tell him, although my words are more like a plea.

"What? You mean like how you did that exact thing to me?"

"I didn't know," I say. The toilet flushes and we both look towards the bathroom door.

"You've got three minutes, Kathryn. Get your shit together or don't come. I really don't give a fuck. But she probably will," he hisses.

I suck in a breath. I never expected a warm welcome from Gray, if I ever saw him again. I destroyed everything we had. But this cold hatred he's directing at me...? I don't think anything could have prepared me for this.

"Don't think for one second I won't take her without you. Because I will," he's quick to add, in case I didn't already believe him.

I walk out of my room and into Graycee's. I pull out a bag and start packing some of her clothes. I don't care if I don't have anything, but my daughter needs her stuff. I then pick up her schoolbag and fill it with some of the books on her shelf. I have no idea how long we're going to be at Gray's.

Until you can run again, is what the little voice in my head answers for me. It's not safe for him to be with us.

Chapter Eleven

I scoop Graycee into my arms, sit her in the back of my truck, and buckle her in. I don't even know if she needs a car seat or something but that's a problem for another day. I'll learn. I'll figure it all out tomorrow.

Then my eyes land on this little girl, who hasn't

even flinched at the fact I'm picking her up and putting her in a strange vehicle. She's too fucking trusting.

My gaze flicks to Kathryn, and a mixture of anger and lust courses through me. I fucking hate her for keeping my daughter from me. I hate her for leaving. For not even giving me the decency of a breakup. Forcing me to wonder for all these years. Thinking she was fucking dead.

I hate her even more for having this effect on my body. I don't want to be attracted to her. I don't want to want her. But, fuck me, when I had her pushed up against that wall, I was torn between hiking up her skirt, shoving my cock into her tight cunt, and following through with strangling her.

I honestly don't know what I would have done if Graycee hadn't interrupted us. I don't even know what I'm doing now. I didn't plan to come here and take them back home with me. I didn't have a plan, if I'm being honest. I just needed to confront Kathryn. But when Graycee asked if I was her daddy, something in me snapped. I needed to take her home and I wasn't going to let anyone or anything stop me.

"This is a really big car," Graycee says.

I smile. "It is a big car. You good? You need anything?"

"I'm okay."

I close the car door and look at Kathryn. "Get in." Then I walk around to the other side and inhale a deep breath. Trying to calm myself down before opening the door and facing my daughter again. I slip behind the wheel and look up into the rearview mirror. "Ready?" I ask Graycee.

She nods her head. When I glance over to Kathryn again, I see that her hands are shaking. She's staring out the window.

"No one is going to save you," I whisper low enough that Graycee can't hear me.

Kathryn returns my glare. "It's not me I'm worried about."

"You think I'm gonna let anything happen to her? You think I can't protect my own kid?" I growl.

She doesn't answer. Instead, she turns her head and stares out the window again. I hit the button to call Vinny, putting him on speakerphone. I want her to hear this so she doesn't get any funny ideas about trying to run.

"Gray, where the fuck are you?" Vinny answers.

"Watch your language. I have a kid in the car," I tell him.

There's a moment of silence before he asks, "What did you do?"

"I need a couple of guys at the house, on rotation," I tell him.

"Who you trying to keep out?"

"No one. I'm keeping people in." I smirk at Kathryn.

"Right. I'll have it arranged," Vinny says, then adds, "Gray, don't do anything you can't undo."

I disconnect the call. It wasn't all that long ago that he was telling me he'd love to kill the woman sitting next to me, and now he's telling me not to do anything I can't undo?

I shake my head. Am I really capable of killing her?

The truth is... I don't know. And that scares me.

I look back at Graycee. She's fallen asleep on the seat. "What's her obsession with King?" I ask Kathryn, and she shrugs.

"He was nice to her."

"He's a fucking asshole. She shouldn't be looking up to a jerkoff like Liam fucking King," I growl.

"She has a mind of her own, Grayson. When she's decided she likes someone, there is no talking her out of it."

"She's too trusting. She shouldn't be letting some strange guy come into the house, pick her up, and put her into his car. Have you not taught her anything about stranger danger?"

"You're not a stranger to her. She's always known about you. I've never given her a reason to not trust her father, Gray."

"No, you just didn't give her the opportunity to actually know him," I snap.

Kathryn returns her gaze to the window. The rest of the drive is quiet. When I pull up to my estate, I see two of my father's men already standing guard. I nod as the gate opens and I drive past them.

"You can't keep us here, Grayson. Graycee has school. She has hockey practice and games. My mom..." Kathryn tears up as her voice dips off.

"I think you've forgotten who the fuck I am. I can and will do whatever the fuck I want. You don't get to call the shots anymore. You lost that ability the day you decided to leave town with a piece of me growing inside you," I tell her before parking the car and killing the engine. "You can come and go as you please. No one is keeping you here. But if you so much as think about taking her and running a second time, I will make sure you never see her again. Got me?"

Kathryn nods her head.

"Good. Now, don't fucking forget it." I jump out

of the car, and as much as I want to slam the fucking door, I don't. I walk around and open the back. Graycee stirs as I unbuckle her seat belt and pick her up. "Shhh, it's okay. I've got you now," I whisper into her ear.

I don't wait to see if Kathryn is following us. I walk inside and up the stairs. Then I open the door to the room right next to mine. Using one hand, I pull the blankets back off the bed and lay Graycee down.

Her eyes flick open and she looks at me with uncertainty. Fear. "Mama?" she cries out.

"I'm right here, Graycee. It's okay. Go back to sleep, baby." Kathryn climbs onto the bed and starts running her hands through our daughter's hair. Soothing her.

I kneel down in front of Graycee. She's staring back at me. "I dreamed of you," she says.

"Yeah? What happened in those dreams?" I ask her.

"You came to school, for Parents' Day. I wanted a daddy for Parents' Day," she says.

My heart fucking breaks. I should have been there for her. I should have always been there. And I would have. If only I'd been given the chance...

"I promise I will never miss a Parents' Day again.

I'll be there, anywhere you want me to be," I tell her. I want to lean in and kiss her little forehead. I don't, though. I hold back. She might be trusting, but she doesn't know me.

"It's okay," Graycee says. "I know you were busy."

"I'm never too busy for you, sweetheart. Never." I push to my feet and send Kathryn one last scathing look before I walk out of the room.

My arm reaches out and snatches my phone off the bedside table, hitting at the screen until the alarm turns off. Rubbing a hand over my face, I force myself to sit up. Only to stop when I see my daughter standing in my bedroom, staring at me.

"Graycee? You okay?"

She nods her head. "I thought you were a dream again," she says.

"It's early. You should go back to bed," I tell her.

"Why are you awake?"

"I have to go to work."

"What is your work?"

This is one question that finally has me smiling. Maybe I can beat her Liam King fascination. I mean, if she's that obsessed with hockey, then surely hearing that her dad is in the NHL has to top some random stranger she met once.

"I'm a hockey player, for the Vancouver Knights. I'm the captain," I say proudly.

Graycee's eyes widen. "So, you know Mr. King then? Can you take me to one of his games?"

Son of a bitch. Way to bruise my ego, kid. I chuckle. First my sister and now my daughter. What is it about this fucking guy?

"I can do better than that, sweetheart. Want to come to morning skate with me?"

"*Now?*" she asks with a huge grin on her face.

"Yep, now. I just gotta get dressed, and you should probably put something on other than pajamas... Do you need help? Should we wake your mom?"

"I'm five. I can dress myself," she says with my

sister's level of attitude, hands on her hips and all. "And we should let Mama sleep. She doesn't sleep much." Then her brows scrunch down and her arms fall to her sides. "Do you think Mama will stop being sad now? Because you're back?"

"Why do you think your mama is sad?" I ask her.

"She cries at nighttime. Sometimes I hear her when I wake up."

I have no idea what to say to that. "How about you go get ready, quietly? And we can let your mom sleep a little longer?"

"Okay, but can we leave her a note? She'll worry if she wakes up and can't find me."

"Sure, I'll write a note for her," I say and watch Graycee run out of the room. I get up and go into my closet, pulling on a pair of sweats, a hoodie, and some shoes.

Then I walk over to my bedside table and grab my wallet and phone. When I walk out of my bedroom, Graycee is walking out of hers with a notebook and pencil. She hands the items to me. "Here. We can write Mama a note on this," she whispers.

I take the notebook and pencil and scribble down a message. Straight and to the point.

Took Graycee to morning skate.

Be back later.

"I'll leave this on the bed," I tell Graycee before creeping into the guest room. Kathryn is out of it. I stop for a second and just stare. There are so many questions running through my head.

Why does she cry at night? Why did she fucking leave? Why does it all bother me so much? It won't change what she did.

Placing the notebook on the bed, I slip back out of the room and take Graycee's hand. "Come on." I guide my daughter into the kitchen and sit her up on the counter. "I'm gonna make a shake. You want anything?"

"Mmm, do you have chocolate milk?" she asks while kicking her feet back and forth.

I smile. "I sure do. It's the best kind of milk." I open the fridge and pull out the chocolate milk. Then I grab a to-go tumbler and fill it to the top before going about making my pre-workout shake. "You ready?"

"Yep. Do you think Mr. King will be there?" Graycee looks up at me with hope in her eyes.

"I'm certain he will be," I tell her, even though it's the last thing I want to say.

"Can I bring my skates?"

"Who goes to an ice rink without skates?" I ask while lifting her down from the counter and setting her back on her feet.

"Mama does. She doesn't like skating," Graycee says.

I want to say that's bullshit. Because I happen to know that her mother loves the ice. But I don't. I keep my mouth shut. I don't know Kathryn. I probably never knew her in the first place.

When I get to The Castle, I take Graycee out to the box and call my sister.

"You're late," she says. "Dad's pissed and your coach isn't all that happy either."

"Come meet me at the box. I need a favor," I tell her and hang up.

"This is amazing. I'm at The Castle. Actually inside!" Graycee jumps up and down excitedly.

"Want to know something?"

She nods her head.

"You are the princess of this castle. All of this is yours," I tell her.

"I'm the princess? Really?" she asks.

"Yep. Although maybe don't tell your Aunt Aliyah that. She's been the princess a really long time. She might not like the idea of being dethroned." I laugh when I see my sister walking towards us.

"I have an aunt?"

"You have an aunt and two uncles. And a grandfather," I tell her.

"Do you think they will like me?" Graycee whispers.

"They will love you." I have no doubt that's true either.

"Gray, what's—oh..." Aliyah stops midsentence when she sees Graycee.

"I remember you. You're Mr. King's friend. Is he here? I want to show him how much better I am now," Graycee asks Aliyah.

"Ah, yeah, I'm sure he'd love to see that. But first

he has to finish up with practice," Aliyah tells Graycee.

I clear my throat to get my sister's attention back on me. "Can you sit with her?"

"Ah, sure," she says.

I bend down to Graycee's height. "This is my sister, your Aunt Aliyah. She's going to sit with you while I run into the locker room to get ready."

Graycee's eyes go from me to Aliyah. "Okay. But... will you come back?"

"Always," I tell her before pushing up to my full height again.

Chapter Twelve

I wake with a jolt. The room is filling with sunlight already. My eyes flick around, from corner to corner, and everything that happened last night sinks in.

Gray...

Bringing us here. To his house.

"Graycee?" I call and jump out of bed. Where is she? She was right next to me. I don't know what time I finally drifted off to sleep, but I was holding my daughter as tight as I could.

I didn't want to let her go. I can't lose her. Everything Gray said last night, about taking her away... I know his threats aren't empty. He'll do it, and he'll do it easily.

I won't let that happen. I've fought to keep her safe, to keep *him* safe too. I'm not going to just let him waltz in and screw everything up.

I reach for the notebook that's sitting on the end of the bed and open it.

Took Graycee to morning skate.
Be back later.

He wrote this. Grayson. I'd recognize his messy scrawl any day. He took her. Just took her to morning skate... Who the hell does he think he is?

Shit. I slide my feet into my shoes and pick up my purse. Then I find my phone. It's almost dead but I call Liliana anyway. I'll look for a charger later.

"Hey," she answers.

"He found us," I rush out. "He found us and he took her."

"Whoa, slow down. Who found you?"

"Grayson," I say.

Liliana lets out a sigh. "Okay, and he took Graycee?"

"He took us both, but I woke up and he's taken her to morning skate. He just took her. Left a note. Didn't wake me up or anything. Just took her." I run down the stairs and find myself in a huge foyer.

I don't even have my car. What the hell do I do?

"Okay, slow down. If he left a note, he's intending on coming back."

"I need to go and get her," I say.

"I think you need to let him have this, Kathryn."

"What?"

"You hid her for five years. He's just taken her to the rink. What you need to do is relax."

"Whose side are you on?" I ask her.

"Yours, always, which is why I'm telling you this. If you try to go down to that rink, I don't imagine it's going to end too well for you, Kathryn. You need to give him space. Let him get to know his daughter."

"It's not safe..."

"You keep saying that, without telling me why. What is it you're afraid of?" she asks.

"I gotta go. I'm sorry I called you so early."

"Kathryn, look. I've been surrounded by men

just like Grayson Monroe for my entire life. So trust me when I say this. He's not going to just give up his child. Not now that he's found her."

"I know," I say before disconnecting the call.

I look around and decide to go back upstairs. I need to find a charger for my phone. I head into Gray's bedroom, which was a huge mistake. Something I've been doing a lot lately it seems. Making mistakes. The room smells like him, the sheets still rumpled from when he got out of bed this morning. But there is a phone charger. I plug my phone in and then do something I really shouldn't do. I snoop.

I pick up the things on Gray's dresser. My brows furrow when I see a photo of Graycee. It's from her hockey club, when Liam King came to coach the kids for the day. A newspaper article. That's how he knew we were here. And it's all he has of her. A faded newspaper article he clipped out and kept. I would feel bad if I weren't so pissed off right now.

I leave my phone to charge and walk back downstairs. I want to go to that stupid arena and get my daughter. That's what I should do. But what if Liliana is right? What if me barging in only makes things worse?

I'm pacing up and down the foyer when the

front door opens. I turn, expecting to see Gray, and find one of his brothers instead.

"Kathryn."

I only met the guy once, but I know exactly who he is. "Vinny."

Did Gray send him here to finish off what he started last night?

No, he wouldn't do that. At least I hope he wouldn't.

"It's been a while." Vinny closes the door. He takes measured steps in my direction.

I instinctively back up and look around for anything I can possibly use as a weapon if need be. There's nothing though. I don't respond.

What am I supposed to say to that?

As if reading my mind, he raises a single brow and pins me with a glare. "Nothing to say?" If he's trying to be intimidating, it's working.

"What exactly do you want me to say?" I ask him.

"How about we start with why you decided to disappear? Why you ripped my brother's fucking heart out and tore it to shreds? Because I gotta be honest... Ever since I heard you were back, I've been racking my brain trying to come up with a reason," he says, taking another step towards me. "And I got nothing, Kathryn."

I shake my head. Even if I wanted to tell him, if I told Gray, I can't. And who's to say they'd even believe me? After all this time? I don't even know if those people are still alive. I don't know if the threat is still here. Around Vancouver. But I have Graycee and I can't take chances with her.

"No? You don't have a reason? Or, no, you don't want to tell me?"

"I can't," I say, hating the fact that my voice cracks at the end.

Vinny tilts his head and stares right into my eyes. I don't know what he sees, but after what seems like forever, he nods his head. "Gray will be back in about fifteen. I'm cooking breakfast. Come on." He walks right past me, and I have whiplash from the sudden change of demeanor.

What the hell?

Like I'm on autopilot, I turn and follow him through the house right into the kitchen. I don't get a chance to sit down before I hear my daughter's voice.

"Graycee!" I yell out to her and turn back, catching her as she runs into my arms. "Oh my god, are you okay?" I pull her back and cup her little face in my hands.

"I'm okay," Graycee says and knits her brows. "Are you okay, Mama?"

"I'm okay. I just missed you," I tell her, hugging her close to my chest. I close my eyes and inhale. I need to calm down. I need to get a grip on this situation and figure a way out of it.

I look up and see Gray standing right behind Graycee, his arms crossed over his chest as he directs a seething glare my way.

Well, you know what? Two can play that game.

I summon as much hatred as I possibly can, which is a lot, seeing as he took my daughter without my permission, and glare right back at him.

I see the corner of his lip tip up slightly, like he finds me amusing.

"Mama, I went to The Castle and Gray said I was a princess now." Graycee pulls away from my embrace and peers over towards the kitchen. "Who are you?" she asks Vinny.

"Graycee, this is my brother. Vinny. Your uncle," Gray tells her.

"Hello, Graycee. It's nice to meet you." Vinny walks over and holds out a hand, but Graycee doesn't touch it. Instead, she steps closer to Gray. Something I find odd. Usually it's me she runs to for comfort.

"Hello," Graycee says quietly.

"I was just about to make pancakes. Do you like pancakes?"

"Chocolate chip pancakes?" Graycee asks.

"Mmm, I think I can whip some of those up just for you." Vinny pivots and walks into the pantry.

Graycee turns back to me. "Mama, I skated with Gray and Mr. King and the whole team."

"Did you?" I ask her.

"Uh-huh, and I got a goal." She smiles wide. "And the horns sounded and everything."

"Wow, how cool," I tell her. "I think it's time for you to go take a bath and freshen up. Come on."

"What about my pancakes?" she whines.

"They'll be here ready when you're done." I take hold of her hand and drag her away.

She peers over her shoulder at Grayson. "You won't eat them all, will you?"

"Me? Never. I'll make sure I save you the best ones," Gray says.

"Okay." With that, she happily leaves the kitchen with me.

I can feel his eyes on us the whole way down the hall. Once I'm in the bedroom, I dig through the bag I packed, find her some clean clothes, and then take Graycee into the adjoining bathroom. I turn on the water for her, wait for it to warm up, and place her clothes on the counter. "Okay, all set, baby," I call out.

Just as I close the door behind her, Gray steps into the bedroom.

"You should have woken me up," I tell him.

"Yeah? And you should have told me she existed," he spits out.

I sigh and sit on the bed. "We can't be here, Grayson."

He looks around. "You're free to go whenever you'd like."

I glare at him. Free to go *without* my daughter. Like I'd ever do that. "As long as Graycee is in this house, so am I. I'm not leaving her, Grayson," I tell him. "You'll have to actually kill me if you want to get rid of me."

"If I could, I would," he grunts. "I've got Aliyah bringing you something decent to change into. We have an appointment with a school."

"What school? What for?"

"Vancouver Prep, to enroll Graycee."

"No. She has a school, Grayson. She likes it there. She has friends there."

"Vancouver Prep is a better school with better security and better friends."

"She's five years old. You can't just come in here

and uproot her life like this. She's just settled into her class. She needs a routine. Stability," I plead with him.

"Once word gets out that she's a Monroe, what she's going to need is security. A lot of it," he says.

"You can't go out in public with her, Grayson. You can't put her at risk like that, put yourself at risk." I stop myself before I say more.

"What do you mean? What risk could I possibly be at?"

"You said it yourself. You're a Monroe. It comes with the name." I cross my arms over my chest.

"What aren't you telling me, Kathryn?" he asks.

"Nothing. Just don't... Just let her get used to this first. Get used to you before you drag her through the media circus that will ensue once you go public with this. You really want paparazzi shoving cameras into her face, taking pictures of her and plastering them all over the television and newspapers?"

The bathroom door opens and Graycee walks out. "Can I have pancakes now?" she asks.

"You sure can." Gray smiles at her. Then he leans down to me. "Whatever it is you're hiding, I'm going to find out."

Chapter Thirteen

"We need to find out why she left," Vinny says. "Something isn't right, Gray. She's hiding something, either to protect herself or someone else."

"She's protecting her daughter," I tell him.

"It's not that. She's hiding something. Find out

what it is," Vinny grunts. "She wants to run again, or thinks she has to at least."

"Yeah, because she's a selfish fucking bitch who kept my kid hidden from me for five fucking years." I pick up the crystal tumbler and throw it across the room. Amber liquid spills down the wall along with shattered shards of glass.

"Why the fuck are you wasting good Scotch?" My father's voice pounds through my head.

"What are you doing here, Dad?" I ask him.

"I came to see my granddaughter. Where is she?"

"I sit up straighter. She's at school. She'll be home in about thirty," I tell him.

Kathryn and Graycee have been here for a week now. The more time I spend with my daughter, the more I fall in love with her. And the more I fucking hate her mother for keeping her from me. I've missed so much. I didn't see her first steps. Hear her first words. I wasn't there to pick her up when she fell down.

How the fuck the kid is so fucking open and accepting that I'm her dad, that everything is going to be perfect now that I'm back, I have no idea. I don't know what Kathryn told her about me. I haven't asked. I've avoided talking to the woman as much as I can.

"Whatever the fuck has crawled up your ass today, get over it. Hit the showers," Dad says before turning to my brother. "Vinny, make him some coffee. He needs to sober up."

"I'm fine," I tell him.

"You stink like a fucking distillery. You're not fine. And you're sure as fuck not going to be around my granddaughter looking and smelling like you do."

The threat of someone else keeping Graycee from me snaps that last thread of rage inside me. I jump up and I stand over my father, something I've never done in my life. "Try to keep me from my daughter. I fucking dare you," I growl at him.

"Right, come on. Let's go." Vinny grabs my arm and pulls me back.

"No one is keeping you from her, Grayson. *Think.* Do you really want her to come home to you like this? Go and fucking sober up. It's the right thing to do," Dad says.

I let Vinny drag me out and up to my bedroom. He shoves me into the bathroom. "Get yourself cleaned up," he says.

"Fuck off." I slam the door in his face.

I'm not drunk, not even a little bit. I'm painfully sober. I can feel fucking everything. Have I had a few drinks? Yes, but I'm not fucking drunk.

I turn on the shower and let the room steam up. I have so much fucking anger coursing through me right now. I don't know what to do with it. Just the thought of Kathryn has the rage boiling to the surface while making my dick hard at the same time.

I switch the water to cold, and by the time I'm finished, I've "sobered up" completely. I walk out into the hallway and see Kathryn strolling into the room she's been sharing with our daughter. I've told her she has her pick of any of the other guest bedrooms but she refuses to leave Graycee. Speaking of...

"Where's Graycee?"

Kathryn pauses and turns to look at me. "Downstairs, with your father," she says.

I stare at her. My eyes travel from her feet up to her face and then back down again. Kathryn has always had a killer body, but somehow it's gotten better. Her dress ends midthigh, and right now, I want nothing more than to hike it up and see if what she's hiding beneath it is as good as I remember it being.

"Come here," I tell her, my cock hardening at the thought of sinking into her.

"Why?" She folds her arms over her chest,

pushing her tits up and causing her cleavage to pop out of the top of her dress.

I walk up, grab her arm, and drag her into my room. Slamming the door behind her. "Because I fucking said so," I tell her. Then I push her front against the door and press into her back. "You used to be so good at following directions, Kathryn. What the fuck happened to the girl who wanted to please me to no end?" I pull her hair away from her neck and lower my lips to her skin.

"Wh-what are you doing, Gray?" she asks.

I wrap one hand around the front of her neck, holding her throat, while my other trails up the inside of her left leg, under the fabric of her dress. "Whatever the fuck I want to do, Kathryn. Because I can." I feel her body tremble and my lips smile without meaning to. She's turned on. She fucking loves this. "Tell me... how many men have you let fuck this cunt over the past six years?"

Kathryn shakes her head. "I haven't."

"Bullshit. I don't believe you," I tell her. When my hand reaches her panties, I push them aside and shove two fingers into her. "Fuck, you're wet. You always did like being treated like my whore." I push in and out of her, rougher than I ever would have been in the past.

Fuck. I drop my hand and remove the towel from my waist. Then I pick her up and throw her onto her stomach on my bed.

"Gray, stop," she says, trying to get up.

"No," I tell her. "You don't want me to stop, Kathryn." Lifting her dress, I grab her panties and tear them down the sides. Then my palm comes down hard on her bare ass.

"Ow. Fuck," she cries out while squirming beneath me. I climb over her. "You're so fucking drenched. Your body is begging me to fill it up." I bite down on her neck.

"No, I'm not. It's not," she says.

"Tell me you want me to fuck you, Kathryn." I grind my cock against her, sliding it between her thighs. "Tell me," I growl more forcefully.

A moan escapes her mouth. "I want you to fuck me."

It's quiet but I hear it. I sit up onto my knees, grab her hips, and pick her up so she's on all fours in front of me. Lining my cock up with her pussy, I thrust into her in one hard motion. Stilling when I bottom out.

Fuck. This was a bad idea. Even knowing as much, I can't stop. I pull out and slam back in again.

My fingers dig into the flesh of her hips. Her cunt is better than I remember.

"So fucking tight," I groan, as pleasure takes over. I pick up my speed, aggressively fucking her.

The sounds coming out of her tell me she's enjoying it too. I fucking hate that she's getting off, and still I find myself wrapping a hand around her waist. My fingers find her clit, and I apply pressure as I rub, exactly the way she used to like me to do it.

"I want to feel your cunt choke my dick, Kathryn. Come for me," I grunt between thrusts.

Her pussy convulses around me. And right before I follow her over the cliff, I pull out, grab my cock in my hand, and squirt my seed all over her ass. When I'm finished, I stand up. Realization sinks in and I fucking hate myself. But I hate her more.

"Get out." I walk over, pick up my towel, and wrap it around my waist.

"You're an asshole," Kathryn hisses as she climbs off the bed.

"Yup. You'd be best not to forget that," I tell her.

"Why? Why do this? You can go and fuck any woman, Grayson. You don't need to do this."

"They're not you, though," I tell her, stepping up until her back presses against the wall. "Don't mistake this for anything it's not. I fucking despise you. I've never hated anyone as much as I hate you right now," I tell her.

"You might hate me, Grayson Monroe, but I know you also still love me. Otherwise you would have killed me by now."

"Love has nothing to do with it. Not when it comes to you, Kathryn. You're here because you're a good mother to our daughter. That's it. And because I'm not a fucking selfish bitch, the kind of person who would take a parent away from a child." I step back and open the door. "Now, get the fuck out of my room."

After throwing on some clothes, I walk back downstairs and find my daughter in the living room with my dad and brother.

"Guess what?" Graycee says while beaming up

at me.

"You asked Pops for a pet monkey and he said yes?" I lift a curious brow.

"No." She laughs. "But that's a good idea. Poppy, can I have a pet monkey?" Graycee gives my dad a look that's hard to say *no* to.

"Sure." He shrugs.

"Only if it lives at his house," I tell her while gesturing a hand to my dad.

"Mmm, that's okay. But guess what?"

"What?"

"I got an *A* on my spelling test. That means I got all the words right."

"Well, of course you did. You're the smartest kid I know," I tell her.

"Are you coming to my practice today?" she asks.

"Try to keep me away. Why don't you go and get ready? Have you eaten anything since school?"

"Yep, Uncle Vinny gave me cookies and chocolate milk." She smiles.

Over the past week, Vinny has managed to win Graycee over with an incessant use of sugar. She's really warming up to the entire family. Like she belongs here. Because she does. She always has.

"Did you save me any?" I ask her.

"Ahhh..." She peers over to the coffee table

where an empty plate and glass sit with barely a crumb in sight. "I can get you some..."

"No, I'm good, princess. Go get ready for practice," I tell her.

Chapter Fourteen

Kathryn

What the hell did I just do? Okay, I know what I did. And his name is Grayson Monroe. So I guess *why* is the real question. He hates me. He's made no secret of that fact since he brought us here. One little touch from him and I gave him my body. At least I didn't come away empty-handed. Gray always had a thing for making sure I finished first. This time was no different. He knew exactly what buttons to press to have me coming on his command.

I inhale and close my eyes. I shouldn't have let that happen. I know that. But, damn it, I was telling him the truth. I haven't slept with anyone since college. Since him. I mean, I had a baby. And I've been avoiding people as much as I can, for fear of being found. I've been missing him for six years and having him touch me...

Well, I can't *not* cave and let myself enjoy that moment. I know he hates me. I know that, but I don't blame him. If I'm honest with myself, I hate *me* too for what I did to him.

He will never get back what I took from him. All those years with Graycee... She will never get them back either. And when I do figure out a way to run again, well, she may never forgive me. But she can hate me if it means she's safe. If it means Gray is safe too.

I don't know what it will take for me to not be in love with that man. I should despise him for the way he's treating me. I can't though—trust me, I've tried. I'm still trying. I called his bluff. Told him that he still loves me, no matter how much he hates me at the same time, and he didn't deny it. Sure, he skirted around the subject. But there was no outright denial. And then a flicker of hope ignited deep inside me. Before I doused it with a heavy dose of reality. It doesn't matter if he loves me. Love doesn't protect you from your enemies. From mine.

"Mama, Gray's coming to practice." Graycee comes running into the bedroom.

"Oh, great. You wanna go freshen up? I'll get your gear ready," I tell her.

"Are you okay, Mama?" she asks me.

"I'm okay, baby. Come on, we don't want to be late."

"Nope, I need to show the boys the new stick skills Gray taught me." She smiles.

The two of them have been messing around with hockey sticks and pucks through the house all week. Her love for the sport came naturally. I never pushed it on her. I always watched the games, always watched *him*. Until she got to the age where she might recognize the name, and then I did that part in secret. And I guess she just fell in love with the game as she got older and could understand it a little better.

I grab her practice bag, and when Graycee finishes in the bathroom, I take her hand and guide her downstairs. I haven't been able to take her anywhere without one of the Monroe goons accompanying me. If I could, we'd be gone already. Something Grayson is well aware of, it seems.

"Graycee, I gotta head off, but you have fun at practice." Gray's father stops us in the foyer.

"Okay, Poppy. One day, I'm going to be a Knight," she tells him.

"I have no doubt," he says, nodding at me as he passes. "Kathryn." It's the most he's spoken to me since we arrived. I don't blame him. I don't blame any of the Monroes for hating me. The only one who has been oddly nice is Vinny.

Which is a puzzle I can't figure out. I swear that first day he came in here wanting to kill me. And then, like a switch, he's now the only one who doesn't pretend I'm not in the room. Or offers some form of fake politeness in front of my daughter.

"You ready, Graycee?" Gray asks.

"Yep." She lets go of my hand and runs up to Grayson. He bends down and catches her. I get teary-eyed every time I see them together. I wish things could have been different. I wish Graycee had always had him in her life. That he always had her.

She whispers something in his ear that I don't catch but his glare lands on me. Gray whispers something back and then sets Graycee down on her feet. "Why don't you go grab a water out of the fridge, sweetheart? Your mother and I will be right there," he says.

"Okay." Graycee runs off in the direction of the kitchen.

"You need to pull yourself together, Kathryn. She's worried about you. Five-year-olds should not be worried about their fucking parents," Gray grunts.

"You're right. They shouldn't. But I'm human, Grayson. I can't just turn off my emotions at the flip of a switch. We can't all be like you," I hiss at him.

"Figure out how," he says and turns around before following the path Graycee took.

Vinny looks from Gray to me. I didn't even see him standing here. "Something happen between you two?" he asks.

I glance back at him. "Yeah, I ran away, not knowing I was pregnant."

"You've had six years to come back. You chose not to."

"Not everything is that simple, Vinny. Not everything is black and white. Sometimes it's gray," I say and walk past him.

"What the fuck is he doing?" Gray curses under his breath.

We're sitting in the stands, watching Graycee's practice. Her coach is having the kids run stick drills. Which, of course, Gray doesn't approve of. "Shh. He's teaching a bunch of six-year-olds, Gray, not an NHL team."

"Well, with this kind of training, none of these kids will play at the college level, let alone make it to the NHL one day," he grumbles before jumping to his feet. "Fuck it."

"What are you doing?" I ask him.

"I'm going out there and teaching those kids something that's actually useful," he says.

"You can't just come in here and take over, Grayson."

"You keep telling me all the things I can't do,

Kathryn. I would have thought you'd get it by now. I can do whatever the fuck I want. No one is going to stop me," he says, then walks out onto the ice. I don't hear what he whispers to the coach but the guy's eyes bug out of his head, which is now nodding up and down like one of those bobble dolls.

"Okay, kids, take a knee," the coach calls out and they all skate over to him. "We have a special visitor, Grayson Monroe. He's the captain of the Vancouver Knights. And he's here to show us some new skills."

"He's my daddy," Graycee announces, with more than a hint of pride.

My eyes widen and I look around the rink. There are a bunch of other parents here. This wasn't supposed to happen. People aren't supposed to know...

"Yeah, right. You wish," a little boy says to Graycee.

Gray takes a step towards the kid and I hold my breath. Please let the man have the common sense to leave it alone. But then I see a flurry of pink land on top of the boy. Graycee just tackled her teammate. Literally jumped on him.

"He is too!" she yells out.

"Ow!" the kid cries. "No, he's not. Get off me."

He shoves Graycee to the side and scrambles back across the ice.

Gray reaches out an arm and scoops her up. I don't hear their exchange, but Graycee nods her head and he places her back on her feet. "Okay, let's practice. I taught Graycee this drill a few days ago, but you're all going to learn it today. Show 'em, baby," Gray says, gesturing towards our daughter.

Graycee grabs her stick and starts running through the routine. When she's done, she spins around and smiles. "I did it!"

"You did good," Gray tells her before turning back to the small group of kids. "Now, let's see what the rest of you can do."

After another twenty minutes, Gray stalks off the ice and sits back down next to me. The kids always get a little free play at the end of each practice.

"I'm surprised you didn't throw that kid into the boards. I mean, even *I* wanted to," I say.

Gray's lips tip up. "Wait for it."

"What?"

"Just watch." He nods to the ice. And my mouth drops open as I watch Graycee check the little boy against the boards. Damn, she hit him hard too. Didn't even try to slow down.

I push to my feet with a gasp. "What did you say to her?"

"I told her to save it for the game." He smiles proudly. Then he cups his hands over his mouth and yells out, "Way to go, Graycee baby!"

She turns back and looks over at us with a huge smile on her face. "Jesus, you're turning her into you," I mutter under my breath.

"At least I'm not a thief," he says, and my entire body stiffens.

"Wh-what?" I ask. Oh god, he doesn't know. He can't. How could he know what I did? There is no way...

"You stole my child, Kathryn. If that doesn't make you a thief, I don't know what does."

I instantly relax. He doesn't know. But he does notice my reaction. Of course he does.

"What did you think I meant?"

"Nothing," I say and return my focus to the kids still playing out on the ice.

Chapter Fifteen

Grayson

The locker room is full of chatter, everyone amping up for tonight. We're three games away from playing in the final round. That Cup is ours this year. I can feel it.

We're all exhausted. The long practices and longer games are grueling, but the energy in here is palpable. "We're going out there and we're going to fucking win," I tell the team.

"Fuck yeah, we are," Luke hollers from beside me.

The rest of the guys cheer and bump gloves as we make our way out to the tunnel. It's a home game. I have Graycee and Kathryn in the family box with Vinny and Aliyah. Graycee was so fucking excited to be here. This is the first game she's been able to attend. The first time I'm actually playing in front of my daughter.

The moment I step out onto the ice, it hits me. I don't look for Kathryn in the stands like I used to. Like every game before. No, instead, my gaze flicks up to the box and I see Graycee standing there with Vinny. Aliyah is next to them while Kathryn is fuck knows where.

I wave and then run through the warm-ups. "You good, man?" Luke stops next to me.

I snap my stick, hitting the puck into the back of the net. "Never been better," I tell him.

"Three more games, Gray," he says.

"Three more games." I nod.

King stops on my other side, his gaze focused up at the box. "I heard Graycee checked a kid and broke his shoulder," he says.

"Where'd you hear that?"

"Your sister. Graycee told her."

"She didn't break the kid's shoulder. Unfortunately," I grunt. "Wish she had. The little shit had it coming."

"We'll have to teach her to hit harder." The fucker grins.

"I'll teach her to hit harder," I tell him. "You already stole my fucking sister, King. You're not stealing my daughter as well."

"There is way too much to unpack with that, Monroe. I know you can afford a shrink. Maybe look into one." King shrugs before skating off.

"He's not wrong." Luke laughs.

"Whose friend are you anyway?" I ask him.

"Yours. But that doesn't change the truth, Monroe."

We're halfway through the third period. Up by two. It's making our opponents sloppy as fuck. And desperate. And when Nashville gets desperate, shit gets messy.

I've had my eye on King the whole ten minutes we've been on the ice together. One of the Jets players seems to have it out for the fucker. I might not love the guy but code is code. And I live by the fucking code. You fuck with one of my players, you're going to have to fuck with me. It's that fucking simple. And right now, I'm just waiting for a reason to throw gloves.

King is facing off. He wins the drop and the puck flies back right into my blade. I rush down the ice, managing to get past two of the Jets defenseman before I snap it to Luke. He hits it into the boards, the puck flies past the net, and King is there within seconds. He maneuvers around the net when that same asshole defenseman pushes out his stick, right into King's skates, sending Liam to the ice. Before he has the chance to get up, I've thrown my stick, shaken off my gloves, and my left hand is fisting the Jets player's jersey. I might be a great hockey player, but I'm an even better fighter. And this fucker is giving me a place to channel the anger I've been keeping bottled up.

My fist slams into his face. Repeatedly. His arms flail out. He gets one or two hits in, but I don't feel a fucking thing. I just keep throwing punches.

When I'm eventually pulled off him, I glance down at the ice to see it stained red. Then I look up at the family box. Aliyah is covering her mouth with a hand. The sight of blood takes her back to that dark place. Back to her fucked-up childhood. But at least she didn't run off, which is progress.

Graycee is banging on the glass. I can see her lips moving and I wish I could hear what she was saying right now. Kathryn is trying to hold her, talking to her. It's the first time I've seen my ex step up to the window. She looks down at me, and our eyes connect. Then I'm taken back too. To a different time. When the only face I wanted to see in the crowd was hers.

The ref escorts me to the penalty box. Five minutes. But the Jets fucker has five for tripping too. Well, that and what looks like a broken nose. I smirk at him as I sit down and admire my handiwork.

The box attendant's eyes bounce between me and my opponent before he tries to stifle his laughter. Clearly, the guy's not a Jets fan. "I need a phone," I tell him.

"That's not allowed." He shakes his head.

"I don't care. I'm the one who'll get the fine. Give me a fucking phone," I yell at him.

He pulls his cell out of his pocket. I take it and dial Vinny.

"Hello?" he answers.

"Put Graycee on the phone," I tell him.

"Gray, what the fuck are you doing? Are you insane?" he hisses.

"Put my daughter on the fucking phone now."

"Daddy, are you okay?" Graycee asks.

I pause. It's the first time she's called me that. She's told people that I'm her father, even seems proud of the fact. But never directed the title at me. "I'm okay, baby. How are you? What's wrong?"

"He was hurting you," she says.

"He wishes." I laugh. "I'm okay, Graycee. You don't need to worry about me."

"I don't want you to get hurt and have to go away again," she whispers.

"That's never going to happen," I tell her, my eyes flicking to the clock. I've got one minute left. "Graycee, I gotta go and win this game. I love you."

"Love you too, Daddy," she says, then adds, "And, Daddy, make sure you hit 'em harder."

I chuckle, disconnect the call, and hand the phone back to the attendant. He pockets it and shakes his head. There're twenty seconds left on the penalty clock and I'm on my feet, ready to get back out on that ice.

"Daddy, you won!" Graycee runs up to me the moment I step into the family box. I had Vinny hang behind. I don't want the press bothering her. Kathryn was right about trying to keep our daughter out of the public eye.

"I did." I catch Graycee when she jumps up into my arms.

"Right, I'm out," Vinny says, clapping a hand down on my shoulder. "Good game."

"Thanks." I walk over and sit down on the sofa with Graycee. "Did you like the game?" I ask her.

"I don't like when you fight. Why do you fight so

much?" She looks up at me with those same green eyes I see in the mirror every morning.

"I'm sorry you had to watch that. But next time, if Daddy is fighting, just turn around. And wait for it to be over."

"Okay, but can't you just say sorry?"

"I have to stick up for my team. It's my job, Graycee."

"What if you get hurt? Will you have to go away?" she asks again.

I look at Kathryn, who is currently holding back tears. I don't know why I care that she's hurting. It shouldn't fucking bother me. "I won't ever leave, Graycee. I just found you. You're not getting rid of me now."

"Promise?"

"Promise." I kiss her forehead and hold her close to my chest as I stand. "Come on, let's get you home."

Kathryn and I walk out, side by side. Almost everyone is gone, except for a few stranglers. The staff parking lot is behind The Castle. No one is supposed to be back here. So, when I see a shadow lurking between a couple of cars where the light post shines down, I hand Graycee over to Kathryn.

"Stay close." I wrap my arms around Kathryn's shoulder and lead her over to my truck while keeping an eye in that direction. And then I see the flash. A fucking photographer. "Get in the car." I open the door, and Kathryn places Graycee on the booster seat.

"They can't have my photo, Gray." Kathryn's voice sounds panicked.

"What do you mean?" I ask her.

"I mean, I can't have my photo in the press," she stresses. "I can't." She's shaking now.

I take hold of her hands. "Hop in the car, and lock the door. It's okay. I got this," I tell her, then add, "And don't let Graycee see," as the door closes them in.

Kathryn nods from the passenger seat.

"Hey, fucker," I call out and rush up to where the photographer is hiding between two cars. "What the fuck are you doing out here?" As soon as I reach him, I snatch the camera out of his shocked hands. Then I smash it to the ground, pick it up, and repeat the process before removing the SD card for good measure. "If I see you again, I'll have you charged. Get the fuck out of here." I throw what's left of his camera in his direction while pocketing the card.

Once I'm back in the car, I take a deep breath. I really wanted to hit the fucker. I didn't. Because, unfortunately for me, that kind of shit has consequences off the ice.

"Thank you," Kathryn says, her voice barely audible.

I throw the SD card onto her lap. "When we get home, we're going to talk about this," I tell her.

Chapter Sixteen

Kathryn

The faint taste of copper hits my tongue. Shit. I look at the nails I was biting on. I've chewed them right down to the skin while running through scenarios in my head. Trying to come up with what I can possibly tell Gray. He's not going to just forget what happened, forget how I reacted to having my picture taken.

How can I explain it to him without telling him... everything?

Just as we pull onto his street, my phone rings, interrupting my frantic thoughts. When I look at the screen and see it's the hospital, my stomach drops.

"Hello," I quickly answer.

"Kathryn, it's Nurse Lacey. You should come by now, if you can. It's your mom... She doesn't have much longer left," the voice on the other end tells me as delicately as it can.

"I'm... I'm on my way," I say and disconnect the call. I turn to look at Gray. "It's my mom. I have to go to the hospital."

He side-eyes me for a second, then nods his head. The rest of the trip is a blur.

I'm actually going to lose my mom. I'm not ready, but is anybody really ready to lose a parent? My father passed away just before I went to college. It wasn't that big of a loss to me. But it hurt.

My mom though? I don't want to lose her.

Gray parks the car, gets out, and picks up Graycee from where she fell asleep in the back seat. "Are we home?" she asks.

161

"No, baby, we're at the hospital. Your mama needs to see your nana," he tells her.

I climb out. I'm numb, but I can feel the wetness on my cheeks. Gray surprises me by taking hold of my hand and squeezing it.

"You can do this, Kathryn. You have to," he says.

I straighten my shoulders. He's right. I have to do this. "I'm not ready to say goodbye to her," I admit.

"I don't think someone can ever be ready to say goodbye to their mother," he says. He never really talked about his own mother when we were in college, other than mentioning that she was dead and that she wasn't the best person.

I walk into my mom's hospital room a few minutes later, with Gray and Graycee beside me. She looks at us and smiles. But I can tell the movement is strained. She tries to talk but no words come out. I drop Gray's hand and rush over to her.

"Shh, it's okay, Mom. You don't have to say anything." I kiss her forehead, grip her hand, and hold on, willing my strength to somehow siphon into her frail body.

I have no idea how long I sit like this, but I hear Gray stand and walk to the door. "Aliyah and Liam are going to take Graycee home," he tells me. "I'll be back."

As soon as the door closes, I lose it. I've been trying to hold it together because Graycee was asleep on Gray's chest. I didn't want her to wake up and see me like this. I hate when she's not with me. But I've seen how the Monroes have taken to her, how much they love her. I also trust that Gray would never let her go with them if he didn't think they could look after her.

The door opens and Gray walks back inside the room. He comes over and wraps his arms around me. "It's okay," he whispers into my ear. "It's okay to let her go, Kathryn."

I shake my head. "I can't. She's all I have. She and Graycee are all I have." My chest heaves with sobs. My mom fell asleep a while ago, and I don't think she's going to wake up again.

"That's not true. You have me." Gray holds me close to his chest, rubbing a hand up and down my back.

"You hate me," I choke out.

"I do, but you were right. No matter how much I hate you, I still love you. I've always loved you, Kathryn."

"It doesn't matter. Because you hate me too, and you should. I messed it all up. It's my fault. I messed everything up. I lost all those years with my mom.

You and Graycee lost all those years together. I fucked up," I cry.

The machines start beeping. Louder. Faster. I pull away from Gray.

"Mom? No, Mom!" I cling to her. I'm desperate. Like if I hold on tight enough, she won't be able to go.

Gray pulls me back as a group of doctors and nurses rush into the room. And it's like I can see everything going on around me, but I can't do anything but stand here and watch it unfold. Gray's arms are tight around my waist, my knees buckle, and my body goes limp. He picks me up and carries me out of the room. He's talking. He's saying something but I don't know what it is.

I wake up in a dark room. My hand fumbles

across the sheets and hits a hard chest. Far too large to be my daughter's. "Graycee?" My throat hurts as the word comes out hoarse.

"She's okay. She's in her bed," Gray says and then a light flicks on.

"What am I doing here?" I ask him.

"You... ah... you wouldn't let go of me, so I stayed until you fell asleep," he says.

I look at him. Why would he do that? Why is he being nice to me?

"I'm sorry. I'll go back to Graycee's room." I shove the blankets off. My head pounds, my eyes are burning, and my heart hurts. My mom is gone. I'm never going to be able to talk to her again. She's gone.

"Stay." Grayson reaches out a hand to stop me.

I pause and turn to peer back at him. "Why?"

"Because if you go in there now, you'll wake her up. Don't overthink it, Kathryn. Just lie down and go back to sleep," he says before flicking off the light again.

I curl up on the bed and face him. I can just make out his profile in the darkened room. "I need to make arrangements. For my mom," I whisper.

"Not right now, you don't. It can wait until morning."

"What do I do?" I ask him.

"We'll call a funeral director. In the morning," he repeats.

"No, I mean, what do I *do*? I can't go to her funeral, Gray," I tell him.

"Why?"

"I can't take risks like that. I can't be seen at her funeral..."

"Why? Who the fuck are you hiding from, Kathryn? You know... at first, I thought it was me, but I've found you. So who the fuck are you hiding from?" His words are hard, firm, but his voice is still quiet.

"It was never you," I tell him.

"Who then?"

I shake my head, even though he probably can't see me. "I can't."

"I can't help you if you don't tell me."

"You can't help me either way."

"I can. If you let me."

"I think it's easier when you just hate me." I sigh. "This... it's harder."

It's so much harder to not just break down and tell him everything right now. I want to tell him. I want to get it all off my chest. But I don't know what he'll do with the information, and I can't put him at risk.

"You just lost your mother. And I'm trying really hard not to be a dick. But you're getting on my last nerve, Kathryn. Who the fuck are you hiding from?" he says, much louder this time.

The door creaks open and light flows into the room. "Daddy?" Graycee calls out.

"Yeah, baby, what's wrong?" Gray asks, sitting up while turning on the bedside lamp.

"Mama wasn't in my room," she says.

"She's here. Come on, climb up."

Graycee toddles over, still half-asleep, and Grayson reaches out and places her between us. Then his alarm goes off.

"You got work," Graycee says.

"I do. How about you go get dressed and come to morning skate with me? Mama's tired. We should let her sleep some more."

"Yes!" Graycee squeals, then wraps her arms around me. "I love you, Mama. It's okay that Nana is asleep now because we have our memories," she tells me.

I hiccup over a sob. "That's right. We have our memories." I kiss her little forehead. "Be good at the rink."

"I'm always good. Besides, I'm the princess of the

castle, and princesses can do whatever they want. Daddy said so." She beams.

"I have a feeling Daddy's going to regret those words one day very soon," I mumble under my breath.

Chapter Seventeen

Grayson

We're almost at The Castle when my phone blasts through the car speakers. I look at the screen and see Luke's name pop up.

"What's up?" I ask him.

"Where'd you go last night?"

"Home. I'm bringing Graycee to morning skate. Make sure everyone in that locker room is decent," I tell him.

"Will do," he says. "Morning, Graycee. How's my favorite princess?"

"Good, Uncle Luke. I'm gonna get goals," she yells out.

"I bet," Luke says. "See you soon." He disconnects the call.

"Daddy, do you think Uncle Liam will play hockey with me?" Graycee asks.

"Liam is not your uncle. Who told you he was?" I grind out the question while attempting to maintain my cool.

"Well, he's Aunt Aliyah's boyfriend and they're going to get married."

"What? They're not getting married," I grunt.

"Uh-huh, Aunt Aliyah even said I can be a flower girl when they do." Graycee's voice is filled with so much excitement. It makes it impossible to burst her bubble. Because that shit ain't happening anytime soon. That fucker is not marrying my sister. Not as long as I have a say in it.

"Did she now?" I mumble, my fists tightening around the steering wheel.

The moment we enter The Castle, I send a quick text off to Luke.

ME:

We're coming in.

LUKE:

Aye-aye, Cap!

I shake my head and pocket my phone. "Graycee, come here, and cover your eyes," I tell her before placing a hand over her face as I push open the door to the locker room. I look around. When I notice all of my teammates are appropriately dressed, I drop my arm.

"Uncle Liam, I'm here. Are you going to play hockey with me today?" Graycee pulls out of my grip and runs over to King.

I stare at him and shake my head. Then I remember we're about to be out on the ice. I hope he's ready, because I plan on smashing him up a bit.

"You know, those murderous looks are meant for the guys on the other team, not your fellow Knights," Luke says.

"I'm going to kill him," I hiss.

"Sure you are, and then you can break both your

sister's and your daughter's heart when they never see him again." Luke smirks.

My head snaps in his direction. "Sometimes I wonder why I'm friends with you."

"Because you're a grouchy fucker and no one else will put up with your shit," he tells me.

"Keep an eye on Graycee for me. I'm gonna go change," I say to King, instead of responding to Luke's smart-ass remark. As much as I hate the fucker right now, I do trust the guy. If I didn't, I wouldn't be letting my daughter anywhere near him. "Graycee, stay here. I'll be right back."

"Okay, Daddy," she says without even bothering to look at me.

All eyes shoot in my direction, and I can't help the smile that comes over my face when I hear her call me that. The rest of the guys have taken to Graycee. Half of them have kids themselves and Graycee's made friends with more than a few of our younger fans in the stands.

I change as quickly as I can and walk back over to my locker. The coaches are talking about plays, while Graycee is standing with my dad at the front of the room with a huge smile on her face and a choco-late milk in her hands.

"There're three games left in the playoffs. Which

means, right now, that Cup is anyone's. We need to win tomorrow night. We need to get the upper hand. Unless you want the Jets stealing it all right out from under your noses. So are you all gonna just let them take it from you or are we going to step the f—" Coach's eyes drop to Graycee. He clears his throat before continuing. "Step up and bring it home?"

"You can say *fuck,* Coach." She grins up at him. "My daddy says it all the time."

My eyes widen and I choke a little on the stale air. *Way to call me out, kid.* My father looks over at me with that expression of silent disapproval only a dad can give you.

"Graycee, we spoke about that the other day. I can say those words. You cannot," I remind her, while the whole team laughs their asses off at my expense.

"But, Daddy, you said I can do whatever I want. Princesses get to do whatever they want. Remember?" Graycee says.

"Well, yeah, within reason. We'll talk about it later," I groan.

"Okay, let's get out there," Coach yells, and the team heads out to the ice.

I bend down and kiss Graycee's head as I pass her. "Stay with Poppy, okay?"

"Okay," she says.

After practice, King, Luke, and I stay out on the ice. Dad brings Graycee out in her gear. I don't think I've ever seen a kid who loves hockey as much as she does. I've watched the other guys bring their offspring to morning skates, but none of them seem to light up the way my girl does whenever she's on the ice.

"Okay, Graycee, we're playing two-on-two," I tell her. "You're with me."

She skates over and holds out her little hand for a fist bump. After touching gloves, she whispers, "Don't worry, Daddy, Uncle Liam always lets me win. We're going to beat 'em good."

"Graycee, baby, I don't need your Uncle Liam to let me win. I can beat him all on my own," I tell her.

Wait... When the fuck did I start referring to the asshole as Uncle Liam?

"I know that, Daddy. You're the bestest player in the NHL," Graycee says with a huge smile on her face.

It takes me aback. The praise from a five-year-old girl means more to me than any other accolades I've received throughout my career. And I've received a lot of them. I didn't accidentally fall into this position. I've worked my ass off to get here. No matter what fuckers like King think about my old man owning the team.

"Well, until you came along. I think you're going to take my title," I tell her.

"I'm not going to be a hockey player when I'm grown up," Graycee says. "I'm going to be like Poppy and own the team. He told me I can pick the players I want that way," she says.

"I don't doubt that, Graycee. Now, are we playing or what?" I ask her.

"Playing!" she yells out enthusiastically. Then she taps the puck over to me before her little legs take off down the ice. When she's in position, with Luke doing a shitty-ass job of trying to cover her, I make a quick pass, and watch as she swings hard, sending the puck right into the back of the net. "Yes! That's how you score goals."

I kept Graycee out on the ice as long as I could. Mostly because she loves it, but also because I'm avoiding having to go home. My mind is fucking confused where Kathryn is concerned. When I saw how destroyed she was over her mother's passing, all I wanted to do was hold her and make everything better. I've never seen Kathryn upset like that before, and it fucking tore at my heart.

Which just pisses me off because I should hate her. I *do* hate her. I hate what she did anyway. But do I hate *her*? As a person? I'm not too sure anymore. Even if I do, it doesn't stop me from wanting to protect her. Like I said, I'm fucking confused as shit.

I also want some fucking answers. I know she's

hiding from someone. And that someone isn't me. I want to know who it is. If there's a threat to Graycee, I want to exterminate it. Fuck, if there's a threat to Kathryn, I want to bury it too.

"Hey, Graycee, how about we get Aunt Aliyah to come over and take you shopping? You need to get some new stuff for your bedroom," I tell her.

"What sort of stuff?"

"Things to decorate, things to make the space yours."

"Okay." She shrugs.

I park the car and call my sister to arrange a little shopping trip. Mostly, I want to be able to talk to Kathryn without worrying that Graycee will over-hear us.

When we walk into the house a few minutes later, Kathryn is still in bed. My bed. "Are you tired, Mama?" Graycee runs in and jumps on top of the pile of blankets on the vacant side of the mattress.

"I'm awake now," Kathryn says. Her eyes are bloodshot from crying.

"Aunt Aliyah is coming to take me shopping. And she's going to make Uncle Liam come too," Graycee tells her mother.

"Uncle Liam? When did that become a thing?" Kathryn asks me.

"It's not a thing," I grunt.

"Aunt Aliyah is going to marry Uncle Liam and I'm going to be their flower girl," Graycee announces with that same enthusiasm she had earlier.

"They're not getting married," I grumble.

"Yep, they are, Daddy. Aunt Aliyah told me so and she wouldn't lie to me."

"No, she wouldn't," I agree. I need to talk to Aliyah about filling my daughter's head with all these ideas about weddings and flower girls. I'm not ready for my little sister to date, let alone get married.

Chapter Eighteen

"I'm sorry. I'll get out of here," I tell Gray shortly after his sister arrives and takes Graycee shopping.

"Stay. We need to talk," he says.

"I need to organize things for my mom." Right now, I'd rather walk through hot coals than talk to

179

Grayson. I know he's going to have questions, and I don't have any answers I can give him.

"I've already called a funeral director. He's coming to the estate this afternoon. But, first, we need to talk."

"About what, Gray? I can't do this. Not today." I jump off his bed and walk out of the room.

The sound of his heavy footsteps follows me into the bathroom I've been sharing with Graycee. I turn on the water, hoping the noise will drown out anything he has to say.

"This conversation is six years overdue, Kathryn. We're having it now, whether you like it or not," he hisses.

I lift my shirt over my head. I really don't care if he sees me naked. It wouldn't be the first time, and I want a shower. I want to make arrangements for my mother. And I do not, under any circumstances, want to have *this conversation* with him.

"There's nothing to say, Gray," I tell him, unclasp my bra, let it drop to the floor, and then undo my jeans and slide them down my legs along with my panties. "I left. I didn't know I was pregnant when I did. And for that, I'm sorry."

"You ran and hid. That's not just leaving, Kathryn. Who are you hiding from?" he asks, his glare briefly straying from my face and skimming across my body before meeting mine again.

I step into the shower and put my head under the running water. I close my eyes. Maybe if I pretend he's not here, he'll disappear. I know it's childish, but desperate times call for desperate measures.

Then I feel the energy shift. I look over and am met by those emerald green eyes that have haunted me for the last six years. Thankfully the shower streams down my face, concealing the tears now forming on my lashes.

Gray reaches up and cups my cheek. "Why? If you left, simply left because you didn't love me, you didn't want to be with me, then just say it. Tell me. Tell me why, Kathryn."

I shake my head. "I can't."

"You owe me this at the very least. What did I do to make you want to leave me?" he asks.

"You didn't do anything, Grayson. It's not you. It wasn't you. I didn't leave because of anything you did. I left because I couldn't bear the thought of anything happening to you if I stayed. I left to protect you. I didn't have a choice," I scream as my palms land on his chest, that firm fucking chest of his.

"What?" Gray takes hold of my wrists. "What are you talking about?"

"It's my fault. I had it all. I had you. I had everything and I ruined it. I did this to us. I know that. I get that there is no going back. I fucked up, Gray. I can't undo what I've done. But that doesn't mean I'm not sorry. Wish there was some way I could take it back. But I can't. I'm just sorry. So sorry." My knees buckle and I fall to the floor.

Gray sits down, inside the shower stall, right in front of me. Placing a finger under my chin, he lifts my face so that our eyes meet. "What did you do?"

"You were right. I'm a thief," I tell him.

"What did you do, Kathryn? Who are you hiding from?" he repeats.

I shake my head. "I can't tell you. They will find me. You won't be safe. Graycee won't be safe." I'm sobbing. My chest heaves as a panic takes over my body.

"Shhh. Graycee is going to be fine. I won't let anything happen to her. She's okay. I'm fine. Kathryn, we're going to be okay." Grayson picks me up and sits me on his lap, my legs circling his waist. He holds my head to his chest and slowly rocks while telling me over and over again how everything is going to be okay.

It's not. It's never going to be okay. I'm always going to be running. I'll always be looking over my shoulder.

I lift my head. My eyes meet Gray's. And the next thing I know, I'm slamming my lips onto his. My arms wrap around his neck. I hold his face to mine as my tongue pushes into his mouth. This kiss is frenzied. I'm desperate for him. There's something inside me that needs him to know that I love him. He was supposed to remember that. He promised he'd remember that.

Gray's hands tangle through my wet hair, his tongue duels with mine, and I feel just as much emotion pouring out of him as what I'm trying to give. I'm already on his lap, but I find myself attempting to get closer. Needing to be closer.

This isn't like the last time when he was so filled with hatred. This is different.

"Fuck." Gray pulls away from the kiss. His eyes bore into mine and the corner of his lips tip up. "I like you better as a blonde," he says and then fuses his lips with mine again.

Gray grabs my hips, lines his cock up with my pussy, and then slowly pulls me down onto him. My head tips back. Having him inside me is a feeling I can't describe. But it's something like coming home.

Being where I belong. A place I never should have left.

His hand grips my chin and his lips find mine again. He swallows my moans as I grind myself on him. Lifting up and down on his shaft. His palms move to my hips and he guides my movements.

"Fuck, you feel so good. Always so fucking good," he groans.

"Mmm, so good," I agree as I slide down his length.

Gray's lips trail down my neck, and I arch my back to give him better access to my body. His mouth then latches on to one of my breasts. "So fucking good," he repeats around a mouthful of my skin. He flicks his tongue out, teasing my nipple before his teeth graze the surface, and he bites down slightly.

"Shit. Oh god." I hold his head in place, not wanting him to stop what he's doing. And my pace picks up as I chase my release.

"Come all over my cock. I want to feel you come for me, Kathryn," Gray growls, his lips traveling back up my chest, along my neck, and then finding my lips just in time to swallow my scream as my body convulses.

My every nerve ending lights up as pleasure

consumes me. That euphoric sensation hits. And I feel like I'm floating.

"Fuck, I'm going to come," Gray says before he thrusts himself deep and his cum squirts inside me.

I still. Look at him. And then jump up and scramble backwards.

"What's wrong?" he asks, his glare bouncing around every inch of my skin.

"You just came inside me, Grayson." My words come out on a rushed whisper.

"It's not like I haven't done it before, Kathryn."

"Yeah, and last time it resulted in Graycee," I remind him.

"Who just so happens to be the best fucking thing I've ever made. Not that I've had much to do with how awesome she's turned out to be," he says, his voice dipping at the end like it always does when he mentions how much he's missed of her life.

I inhale, trying to steady myself. "I'm not on the pill."

"Okay. Well, at least if I knock you up again, you won't be able to run off this time." Grayson pushes to his feet, and I feel a sudden chill that has nothing to do with the water turning cold. "The funeral director will be here in twenty minutes," he says.

My mom. For a few minutes, I'd let myself forget.

I nod my head and watch as Grayson steps out of the shower and wraps a towel around his waist. "When did you get my name on you?" I ask when my eyes land on the tattoo scrawled across his ribs.

He glances down, almost as if to make sure it's still there. "When I accepted the fact that you were dead, because I couldn't for the life of me think of another reason you'd leave me," he says before walking away.

"I'm sorry," I call out to his back.

"Yeah, me too," he says over a shoulder, quickly closing the door on me and what's left of this conversation.

After pulling myself together as best I can, I walk

downstairs. I have no idea where the funeral director is meeting us. I head for the games area, because that's where Gray usually hangs out. When I walk past the living room, the voices that float through the door have me stopping in my tracks and turning in that direction.

"Lil? What are you doing here?" I rush over to my best friend—well, at least she was at one point. Now, it's just another relationship I destroyed with my actions.

"Why wouldn't I be here? I heard about your mom. No thanks to Grayson." She shoots the man in question a glare that would send many people running. Though he appears unaffected.

"You want me to tell you shit, Lil? Maybe you should have given me the same fucking courtesy six years ago when you helped her run off with my kid," he grunts.

"First, I didn't know she was pregnant. Neither did she by the way. And second, she's my best friend. You really think I wasn't going to help her?" she fires back.

Gray folds his arms over his chest, leaning against the door, while clearly refusing to answer Liliana's question.

"I'm sorry. You two should not be fighting

because of me. Gray, I did this, not her. It wasn't her fault," I tell him.

He looks at me, and his eyes soften ever so slightly. "The funeral director is waiting in the dining room. Just tell him what you want. I've already written him a blank check," Grayson says and walks out.

I want to go after him. I want to fix this, but it is easier if he's angry at me. It hurts more when he's the same sweet, caring man I remember.

"You two are totally banging again," Liliana hums, and my neck snaps in her direction.

"What? Don't be ridiculous. Did you not just see how much he hates me?"

"Yep. But there's a fine line between love and hate. And you two have crossed it." She smiles.

"Shut up." I roll my eyes.

"So... was it good? Same as it used to be? Or better? I mean, Lord knows that man has had a lot more practice while he's been waiting for you to come to your senses," Liliana says.

I suck in a deep breath. I know I don't have a right to be jealous at the thought of Gray with another woman. I was the one who left. Not him. But it still stings.

"Come on, let's not leave this guy waiting," I say instead of replying.

Liliana links her arm with mine. "If he hates you so much, why is he paying for your mother's funeral?"

And just like that, I'm reminded why my best friend is here as a fresh wave of tears bursts free. I can't do this. I can't plan a funeral. I can't even *go* to a funeral. What am I supposed to tell the director? Just bury her, because she won't have any family there anyway?

"I can't..." My hand claws at my throat as my lungs fight for oxygen.

"Shit. Kathryn, it's okay." Lil hugs me. But I push away from her.

"It's not okay," I heave, still fighting for air.

"Fuck. Grayson!" Liliana yells out.

And before I realize what's happening, Grayson has his hands on my face. "What the fuck did you say to her?" he growls at my best friend.

"I can't..." I heave again. It's like my body has forgotten how to breathe.

"Shh, babe, it's going to be all right. You're going to be okay." Gray tugs me into his chest, and my hands cling to his shirt, twisting the fabric between my fingers.

"I can't... the funeral," I tell him.

"You can do this. Look at me." He pulls me back by my shoulders. "Look at me," he repeats. When my eyes meet his, I don't see hatred anymore. I see concern. "You are stronger than this. Come on, we can get through this."

"Grayson, I can't be at her funeral," I sob.

"I'll figure it out. You're not missing your mother's funeral. Come on, let's go talk to the director." He takes my hand, before Liliana takes hold of the other one.

God, I wish I could go back in time. I should have come up with another way to pay for college. I was so stupid. One bad decision and I lost everything...

Chapter Nineteen

Grayson

"How do you do this all year?" I grumble to Franco. He's one of the centers, a veteran player with four kids of his own at home.

"Do what?" he asks.

"Be away from your kids so much?" I'm really

fucking struggling with the fact I left Graycee behind for this game.

"I'd tell you it gets easier, but it doesn't. You just take it one day at a time," he says.

"Yeah." I might have to convince Kathryn to get on board with homeschooling. At least then Graycee could come on the road with me.

"You worried she's gonna try to run?" Luke chimes in.

"I'd be an idiot if I wasn't. She wants to do it. I can see it in her eyes every time she looks at me," I tell him. I have ten of my father's guys at the house, following Graycee around. There is no way Kathryn is going to be able to take off with my daughter this time around.

I might have also put a tracker in Graycee's backpack and her hockey gloves. I'm not taking chances. I tried to put one in that fucking puck Graycee treats like the Crown Jewels. The one King signed for her. But the tech guy couldn't do it without damaging the damn thing.

"Two games left. If we win this one, that trophy is ours. Get out there and play like your life depends on it," Coach yells out, forcing all of our attention back on the ice.

We're on game four out of five. We've won two

of the three we've played so far. I need to shake thoughts of Graycee out of my head and focus on my job. It'd be better if I could trust Kathryn not to try to take off again. I don't. I'm not sure I ever will. She still hasn't told me what the fuck is going on or who the fuck she's running from. I've got Vinny staying at the house. He's been building her trust over the last few weeks. The fucker is just as determined as I am to find out what she's hiding from us.

I step out onto the ice. We're at the Jets' home base, and you can tell from all the red in the stands. King is at the puck drop, while I've got one of the opposing assholes on me.

"I heard your sister's fair game now. Word is you let King have her first, and now the rest of the team is taking turns. I'll have to get my agent to work on a trade. Looks like the benefits of being a Knight are getting better by the day," the fucker says.

I look at him. *Is this prick for real right now?*

I straighten my spine as my stick drops to the ground. "Okay, asshole, you really want to do this? Let's do it." My gloves land on the ice and the fucker in front of me does the same.

His arm swings out. I duck and grab a fistful of his jersey in my left hand while my right connects with his face. I only get four hits in before I'm being pulled off.

"Five minutes for roughing," the ref announces the penalty, then we're each escorted to the box.

The Jets player smirks at King as we pass him. "That tight Monroe princess ass is going to feel good when I shove my cock into it."

I push off the ref and immediately head for the fucker again. By the time I get there, King's gloves are off and he's beating me to the punch. I join the chaos, pulling the guys off King's back and tossing them onto the ice with a thud.

When the fight is finally broken up again, King gets a five-minute penalty and we're down two players while the Jets are down only one. Fuck!

The moment we're shoved into the penalty box, my eyes flick over to the fucker sitting on the other side of the glass, smiling from ear to ear with his split fucking lip dripping blood down to his chin. Then I return my focus to the game.

"They're gonna go after Luke," I tell King. We're not out there to defend him, which leaves our guys open. And, sure enough, that's what the Jets do as soon as they get the chance. Luke's not stupid though. He anticipates every hit. "When we get back out there, this fucker is going down."

"Lead the way, Cap." King smiles.

When there's thirty seconds left on the penalty clock, King and I are both on our feet, ready to get right back out there. The Jets are up by two. That power play gave them an advantage. Something I now know they planned from the get-go. Fucking idiots. I'll make sure they regret the stunt they just pulled.

My skates hit the ice and I head for the puck. Luke anticipates my movements, passing to me. I'm in a perfect position for a goal, but an even better position to teach that asshole Jets player a fucking lesson. I snap my stick back and hit the puck, sending that little black disk flying through the air. It nails my intended target with an audible crack, and I smirk as the son of a bitch hits the ground with blood streaming from his face.

Maybe next time he'll think twice before talking shit about my sister.

"It's okay that you lost, Daddy. You'll get 'em next time," my daughter says through the phone.

I'm lying on the hotel bed, wishing like hell I could be at home with her. Video calls are not the same as having her with me. "I know, baby. What'd you get up to today?" I ask her.

"I went to school, then practice. And then came home. Mama is still sad," Graycee says.

"I think she misses your nana. It's okay for her to be sad about that. How was practice?"

"I checked Adam into the boards, just like you showed me, and he called me fat," Graycee huffs.

"He what? That little shithead," I growl into the phone. "Graycee, you are not fat. Far from it."

Fuck, why is it frowned upon for a grown-ass man to beat the shit out of a little kid? I'd really love to teach that fucker a lesson.

"That's what Mama said," Graycee replies.

"You are the most beautiful girl I've ever seen in the entire world, sweetheart."

"What about Mama?" she asks.

"What about her?"

"Do you think she's beautiful too?"

I pause. I don't want to give Graycee the idea that there's anything between her mother and me. But I also won't lie to the kid. "I think she's the second most beautiful thing I've ever seen," I say honestly.

Graycee laughs. "She says that too."

"What does she say?" I push myself up on the bed, like that somehow helps calm the too-fast beating of my heart. It doesn't. I shouldn't want to hear anything Kathryn has to say about me. But I do. It doesn't matter how much time has passed; that woman still has her claws in my chest.

"That you are beautiful. And that you have amazing eyes like me."

"She said that, huh? Well, you do have pretty amazing eyes," I say before quickly switching topics. "So, tell me. How are we going to teach this Adam fucker a lesson? We can get Uncle Vinny to go talk to him tomorrow. Scare him a little."

"No, Daddy. I already punched him in the face."

"You did what? Graycee, you should not be punching anyone," I tell her.

"But you do it."

Shit, she has me there. "That's different. I don't want you fighting. You're better than me."

"I think you're the best. I'm really glad you're my dad and that you found me." I can hear her smiling into the phone, and now my chest hurts more.

"Yeah, me too." I sigh and Graycee yawns. "It's getting late. You should hop into bed."

"Okay, good night. I love you."

"Love you too, sweetheart." I hang up the phone, close my eyes, and inhale while ignoring the knock on the door.

Until whoever it is starts banging louder.

"Fuck, okay, I'm coming," I yell out. Swinging the door open, I find Luke and King on the other side. "You fuckers lost?"

"Nope, we got food." Luke holds up a bag of McDonald's.

"There better be cookies in there or ya might as well turn your asses around and go back," I tell him. McDonald's cookies are underrated in my opinion.

"There is." He sets the bag on the table. We each pull a chair over before Luke starts handing out burgers and fries and then rations out four packets of cookies. I swipe up two of those fuckers.

"That was a fucked-up game," King says.

"You don't say?" I look at him, sarcasm dripping off my words. "You know what else is fucked up?"

"What?"

"This idea my daughter has that you're marrying my sister."

King smiles. The fucker has a fucking huge-ass smile on his face. Like this shit is funny. "Oh, I'm definitely marrying your sister," he says.

"Okay... before you get all big brother, *don't touch my baby sister* on us, think about what you're doing. If Aliyah, for whatever reason unbeknownst to us, wants to marry this asshole, then you have to find a way to make peace with it," Luke says around a mouthful of burger.

"Stop playing fucking Switzerland and pick a side." I point at him.

"Right now, I'm on Team Luke." He gestures to himself before motioning between King and me. "You all can duke it out till only one of you is left, for all I care."

"Find anything on the Kathryn front? What is she scared of?" King asks, quickly changing the subject.

"Not a fucking thing," I grunt, pick up a fry, and bring it to my mouth.

"Something had to have spooked her. Still spooks her. She's constantly looking over her shoulder, literally," Luke says.

"I know. But what can I do about it if she won't tell me?" It's not like I can get Vinny to pull the information out of her. Not the mother of my child, with the methods he uses.

"What about her friend? Liliana?"

"She's too loyal, and not someone you want to piss off unless you want her entire family coming after you. And, trust me, you do not want to be on the Valentinos' shit list," I groan.

"Have you asked your dad to help?" Luke questions.

"No."

"Maybe you should." He shrugs.

"Vinny is trying to find out. He's practically Dad 2.0," I say.

"But he's not your father. You never know. I mean, your dad and uncle have a lot more reach."

"Yeah, I might ask him to look into it. That's if he hasn't already," I tell Luke.

It is a little odd, come to think of it, that my dad hasn't said much about Kathryn's return. He's over the moon about being a grandfather and having Graycee around. He dotes on her just as much as he did on my sister when she was little. Still does with Aliyah. But he hasn't said a single thing about Kathryn. Which has me curious as to why that is.

"Hold on," I say, get up, walk over, and pick up my phone. I dial my dad's number and wait for him to answer.

"Grayson," he says.

"Dad, what do you know about Kathryn's disappearance?" I ask him. There's a silence on the other end of the line for a good minute. I pull the phone away from my ear to check that the call is still connected. It is. "Dad?"

"Nothing, Gray. Why would I know anything about that?"

"No idea. Just weird how you haven't had anything to say about her being back... is all."

"That girl broke your heart, Grayson. I'm not going to throw her a fucking welcome back party anytime soon. She also stole a piece of our family. So forgive me for not sparing her a second thought," he snarls.

"Why do you think she left?" I try again.

"I don't know. Maybe you should ask her," he says.

"I have."

"And?"

"And she said something about not wanting to get me into trouble or some shit," I tell him.

"Why would you be in trouble?" he asks the same question that's been plaguing my mind.

"No idea."

"Okay. I'll look into it," he says.

"Thanks, Dad."

"Grayson, you better clean up your act by the next game. I want that fucking Cup."

"You and me both," I grunt, cutting the call before I throw the phone back onto the bed.

Chapter Twenty

"**D**addy's coming home today!" Graycee is practically jumping out of her skin with excitement. Me? Not so much.

I've been trying to figure a way out of this place in his absence. I haven't been so lucky. Everywhere I looked, he's had one of his father's goons watching me.

"Yeah, he is. I bet he's just as excited to see you," I tell her.

"You think he misses us?" Graycee asks.

"I know he misses you, baby. Come on, let's get ready for school."

"I don't wanna go. Can't I stay home and wait for Daddy?" She tries using those doe eyes that work so well on her father *on me*. Difference is I've grown immune to them over the years.

"No, you can't. I'm sure by the time school's out, he'll be here waiting for you," I tell her.

After I drop Graycee off, I head back to Gray's house. I feel so lost during the day when she's not with me. When I was at my mom's place, I had things to do. Cleaning, cooking, little things around the house. I was even beginning to sort through Mom's stuff, knowing the end was near. I kept busy. Before that, I was always working two and three jobs. Trying to make ends meet. Struggling to pay the bills and keep a roof over our heads.

Here though? I don't know what to do here. Grayson has people to do all the little things for him. For us. And right now, I feel useless.

"Hey, Graycee at school?" Liliana asks from where she's standing by the bedroom door. I didn't even hear her sneak up on me.

"Uh, yeah, what are you doing here?" I thought she went home.

"Well, gee, it's freaking great to see you too." Her face scrunches up—she's teasing me—and her body flops next to mine on the bed.

"You know I didn't mean it like that. I just thought you went home. Also, how'd you get in here? This place is locked down tighter than Fort Knox," I tell her.

"Yeah, it's almost as bad as my house," she says. "But when your last name's Valentino, doors kind of just open for you." She laughs. And then rolls over to face me.

I've been in such a slump since my mom died.

All I've been doing is lying in bed, until it's time to pick Graycee up from school. Once I have her, I'm busy doing homework, playing games, going over her day, ushering her through bath time, and managing the rest of our daily routine.

"How are you?" Liliana asks.

"I'm fine." I sigh.

"No, you're not. Talk to me, Kathryn. If you keep holding this in, it's going to eat you up from the inside out."

"I don't know what you want me to say, Lil. I'm stuck in this place." I wave a hand around the room. "There's no way out. Trust me, I've looked. And I know it's only a matter of time before they find me..."

"Before who finds you?"

"You know I can't tell you that." I shake my head.

"How do you know the situation is as bad as you say it is? I mean, it might not be. If you tell me, I can help. We can figure it out. You deserve your happy ending, Kathryn."

"I don't deserve anything," I say, and I mean that. "I can't undo what I did."

"Did you kill someone?" she asks.

"What? No, I didn't kill anyone." I furrow my brows at her.

"It'd be okay if you did. I have a contact for

cleaners." She shrugs. Sometimes I guess I forget *who* she is. I mean, I know who she is. But knowing and *knowing* are two different things. Even if that doesn't make all that much sense.

"Wow. So you wouldn't help me bury the body? You'd just get rid of it altogether?"

"Exactly. Buried bodies can be found. Bodies that don't exist? Not so much."

"I'm really glad you're my best friend. Well, that you were. I don't expect that title now. But you know what I mean," I ramble on.

"Kathryn, stop. I love you. I don't care what you did. I don't care how long it's been since we saw each other. *I love you.* And whatever it is? Trust me when I say it's not as bad as what you're making it out to be in your head."

"Maybe."

"I know I'm right, and you know I'm right too," she says. We lay here in silence for a while before Liliana jumps off the bed. "Okay, I've given you enough time. Come on, get up."

"Why? What for?"

"Makeover time. Grayson's coming home today, and when he does, you're going to blow those skates right off his feet." She smiles.

"Ah, no, I'm not."

"Yes, you are. Gray is your happy ending, Kathryn. I just know it, always have."

"I'm the villain in this story, Lil. I don't get the guy. I don't get the happy ending."

"Bullshit. What kind of whacked-out fairy tales did you grow up reading? Everyone loves a good redemption arc. I mean, who wants to read about perfect characters? Our flaws make us interesting. Besides, everyone knows the villains are way more fun."

"I really do worry about you sometimes," I tell her as she reaches for my hands and pulls me up off the bed.

"Just... let me have this. We have not had a spa day together in six years, Kathryn. I need it. You have no idea how many puck bunnies Travis has chasing him after every game. I need to keep up this appearance so he doesn't go looking elsewhere."

"You're kidding, right? He'd be a fucking idiot to look elsewhere."

"Oh, I know, and I'd cut off his dick before I made him choke on it. Rumor has it my Zia Angelica did that to a guy once, you know?" Lil smiles proudly. "She's the best."

"I'm sure," I tell her as a shiver travels down my

spine at the thought. The Valentinos are a different breed.

Before I know it, I'm sitting in a chair with a cape around me and a stylist fluffing out my red locks.

"Love the red, but also... *don't*," the guy currently holding my hair says as he combs a hand through the ends.

"Right. It's not bad, but she's a natural blonde," Lil tells him.

"Okay, let's get to work. And don't look so scared, honey. I'm James and I'm going to transform you from a simple *wow* to a *sweet baby Jesus*," he says to me.

I look to Lil, who is sitting in a matching chair next to mine. "Really, Lil? I can't be blonde again," I remind her.

"Nonsense. Just relax. If you don't like it, you can always change it back later." She hands me a glass of champagne before offering a loud, "Cheers!"

"Cheers," I repeat, tapping my glass with hers and then setting it on the table in front of us.

"You know you're supposed to drink that, right?" Liliana says.

"I know. But I have to pick Graycee up in a few hours."

"Actually, I messaged Gray and told him he had

to grab her from school because we were busy."

"You did what?" I screech. "You can't do that." I reach for my phone, swipe it off the table, and call the number Gray gave me. I haven't called him once since he swept back into our lives, and every time he calls me, I've handed the phone straight to Graycee. It's her he's calling to speak to anyway.

"Hey, what's up?" he answers and his voice goes right through me.

"You don't have to pick Graycee up from school today. I can do it. I'm sorry. Liliana shouldn't have asked you to do that."

"What are you doing?" he asks.

"Nothing I want to be doing," I groan.

"What are you doing, Kathryn?" he repeats.

"I'm at your place, sitting in a chair with a stylist Liliana insists I need."

"You're right. You don't need it. But it's fine. I've got Graycee. I'll take her to her practice after school and then bring her home. Besides, I've got a bone to pick with a little fucker who called my daughter fat."

"You can't hit a kid, Gray," I remind him. Because something tells me I need to.

"So everyone keeps saying. I'm not completely unhinged, Kathryn. Relax." He cuts the call.

"Well? What'd he say?" Liliana smiles while

trying to hide it by bringing her glass of champagne to her lips.

"Fuck it," I mutter and pick up my own glass. The bubbles hit my tongue, followed by the sweet, sweet flavor I just now remember. "Oh god, this is good."

"I wouldn't bring over shit champagne," she says. "Now, sit back, relax, and let poor James here do his job."

Four hours later, I'm staring at myself in the mirror. Well, not at myself, but my old self. It's like Liliana showed the stylist a picture of who I used to be, because they've turned me back into that girl.

"Welcome home, Kathryn." Liliana wraps her arms around me from behind. Her lips brush my cheek.

"I can't be this version of me. It's not safe," I whisper.

"Look around you. Do you really think anyone is getting into this place? You are safer here than you've ever been out on your own."

I hear Graycee's squeals coming from downstairs and jump up. "Graycee's home. Come on, let's make sure her father hasn't been arrested for beating up a kid," I tell Liliana.

"He's not that crazy," she says.

I side-eye her. "The kid called Graycee fat at practice the other day."

"Oh shit, RIP, kid." Lil makes the sign of the cross on her body, and I fold my arms over my chest and glare at her. "What? The little shit had it coming." She shrugs.

"I really, really worry about you sometimes." I shake my head.

"So you've said." She links her arm with mine and we make our way downstairs, where we find Gray and Graycee in the kitchen, both sitting at the counter with a huge glass of chocolate milk between them.

I smile at the scene. There are moments when I want my daughter to myself. To just be mine again. I know it's selfish, but I'm not used to sharing her with so many people. However, when I see her with her father, it makes my heart swell. She deserves this. She deserves him. And he deserves her too.

"Mama, you look pretty. You fixed your hair," Graycee says. She's only ever seen pictures of me as a blonde. But this girl doesn't forget anything.

"Thank you, baby. And, yes, I did." I walk up and kiss the top of her head. "How was school?"

"Boring," she grumbles.

"Okay, and how was practice?" I ask her.

"So good. You should have been there. Daddy threw Adam all the way across the ice into the net." She giggles.

My eyes widen before shooting over to Gray, who is staring at me like he's seeing a ghost. I guess, in a lot of ways, he is. "You didn't assault a kid, Grayson, did you? Tell me you didn't."

"I didn't touch the little fucker. He tripped over my stick. That's all." Gray smirks.

"It was great. Adam cried like a baby," Graycee announces with a matching grin. Peas in a pod, these two. And not in a good way.

"Graycee, that's not nice. We don't get joy out of seeing others get hurt," I tell her.

"Sorry, Mama."

"Hey, Graycee, Aunt Lil got you a present.

Come on, let's go find it. I left it in this big ol' house somewhere," Liliana says, picking Graycee up from the chair and walking out of the kitchen with my daughter in tow.

Gray is still staring at me. Hard. I do my best not to squirm under his scrutiny. It's no easy feat, though. "How was your flight?" I ask him.

"Long," he says, pushing up from the counter to tower over me. He tilts his head, his eyes squinting as he stalks forward. "How was your day?"

"Long," I parrot him.

He leans in and buries his face in the crook of my neck. "You look good. Almost like the girl I used to love."

I suck in a breath, too frozen to move a muscle, until he pushes away from me and walks out of the room.

I close my eyes, willing myself not to cry. His words aren't anything I don't deserve. I broke his heart. That's not something I can ever take back or undo. I have to pay for my sins, and if this is my punishment, then so be it. Because at least he's here to dish it out. The alternative...

Well, that would be worse than anything this man could ever do to me.

Chapter Twenty-One

I've been tossing and turning all fucking night. I can't get Kathryn out of my damn head. The way she looked when I saw her this afternoon. Liliana didn't just give her a makeover. She turned back time. It was like stepping into the past. When things were easier, lighter. When I didn't feel this weight on my chest, this anger that just doesn't go away…

I didn't notice it at the time, but it was easier to hate Kathryn when she didn't look like how I remembered her. She was still beautiful. Fuck, I don't think the woman could ever not be beautiful. But when I saw her looking like the girl I fell in love with, the girl I mourned for six fucking years, my heart stopped beating.

"Daddy, you awake?" Graycee jumps on my bed.

"I am now, baby. What's wrong?" I ask her.

"Mama said we have to say goodbye to Nana today," she says.

"Yeah, we do." I sigh. "Come here." I hold my arm out and Graycee snuggles in next to me. "Does it make you sad?"

"I liked Nana," she says.

"You know, just because you can't see someone anymore, it doesn't mean you can't talk to them. If you talk, Nana can hear you."

"Like when Mama would talk to you?"

"Your mother used to talk to me? About what?"

"Mmm, I don't know, but she used to say sorry a lot. She'd say it all the time at bedtime."

"Yeah, just like that."

"Will you get my name on you too one day? You

have Mama's name but not mine," Graycee asks as her tiny fingers trace over the tattoo on my ribs.

"I didn't know how to write your name. So you'll have to write it down for me, and then I'll take it to the tattoo shop and get it copied right here." I tap my chest. "Over my heart."

"Why on your heart? Won't that hurt?" She screws up her little face like she just bit into a lemon and I laugh.

Pretty sure the ribs hurt a lot more, kid.

But I don't say that aloud. Instead, I tell her, "I want it on my heart because you're the only girl in the world to have all of my heart, Graycee. Besides, your dad's a hockey player, and we're tough. I won't even feel it."

"That's true."

"We should get up and get ready." I stretch my arms over my head with a yawn.

"Okay, Aunt Aliyah got me a dress, shoes, and boots," Graycee says.

"Did she now? When?"

"The other day. She came over when you and Uncle Liam were gone."

A few minutes later, I'm walking into the kitchen to meet the girls, only to pause in my tracks when my eyes land on Kathryn. "Is that Versace?"

"Your sister bought it," she groans.

"Of course she did." I shake my head before turning to Graycee. "You ready?" I ask Kathryn.

I'm doing my best not to observe how good she looks in the skin-tight black dress she's wearing. It has a high neckline with big puffy sleeves, but it's the way the material hugs her hips and thighs that makes my eyes drift and almost beg her to turn around so I can see how it looks from behind. She left her hair down, styled in loose curls. Long, blonde, loose curls. Exactly how she used to wear it in college. When I meet her eyes, they're not the same light-blue I remember. Sure, the color's the same. But they're duller now. Kathryn lost that light she used to have.

She could probably say as much about me. I've looked at myself in the mirror enough to know it's true.

"I don't think I'll ever be ready for this," Kathryn says.

I grip Graycee's palm in one hand, place the other on the small of Kathryn's back, and lead them out to the waiting SUV. I arranged to have the funeral home closed off to the public. No one can get in or out. The car windows are tinted, meaning no one can see inside either. It was the only way I could think of to get Kathryn to attend her mother's service.

It's only us. My family, Kathryn, and Graycee in attendance. Then her mother will be cremated.

Once we're all seated inside the SUV, I reach over and grasp Kathryn's hand. She doesn't look at me, but she does hold on. Tight. I can feel her body tremble. I don't know if she's upset because of what today means to her or if she's scared of being seen.

"I was thinking... After the game, we could take Graycee on a trip somewhere. A vacation."

"A vacation? Where?" Graycee asks.

"Wherever you want to go," I tell her.

"Disney?" She's bouncing in her seat already. I take in the excitement on her face.

"Have you been to Disney before?"

"No. Have you?"

"I have, but it was a really long time ago," I tell her. "Okay, so Disney, it is. It's settled."

"Gray, she has school. We can't just take her out of school to go gallivanting around a theme park," Kathryn whispers in my direction.

"We can and we are. It'll just be a week. And she's smart—brilliant actually. A week away from school isn't going to hurt her."

"It's not like I have any say over what happens anyway. You're just going to do whatever you want with her," Kathryn snaps at me.

"Yeah? Where the fuck was my say for the last six years, Kathryn?" I hiss in reply.

"No!" Graycee yells out, and Kathryn and I both look across to her.

"What's wrong?" I ask.

"You're mad," Graycee tells me.

"I'm not mad. I'm upset," I try to explain. Though I guess, to a kid, it all sounds the same.

"I don't like it," she says.

"I'm sorry, Graycee. It's okay. We're okay," I assure her.

She doesn't say anything. She looks at her

mother, just stares at her mother for a few seconds. "Mama isn't okay."

"I *am* okay, baby. I'm just sad about Nana," Kathryn says.

"We don't have to go on a trip, Mama. It's okay."

"It'll be fun. You will love Disney. Besides, Daddy is right. You're way smart enough to miss a week of school and not fall behind," Kathryn tells her.

The rest of the drive is filled with tension. Between Kathryn and me. Between me and the world. And even between me and myself. Though I'm not sure why. I wasn't in the wrong here. I'm the one who has all the lost time to make up for. I'm the one who missed five years of family vacations. Not Kathryn.

When we finally pull up to the funeral home, I'm almost relieved to be getting out of the car. I see everyone out and get stopped by my father the moment we enter the building. Kathryn takes Graycee to the front of the room and sits down with her. The funeral director approaches them and my eyes flick over to the casket, looming in the middle of the... is it an altar? Stage? I don't know. I was never one for church and all the religious stuff. Whatever it's called, the casket is in the middle of the platform, covered in pink and white flowers.

"How is she?" Dad asks.

"Not good," I tell him, my glare still glued on Kathryn and the funeral director.

"How are you?"

"I'm fine," I say.

"Okay."

"Did you find anything out?"

"Nothing," he grunts.

"Well, thanks for looking." I rake a hand through my hair before I can stop myself and make my way to the front of the room. My sister and Liam fucking King are sitting in the row behind Kathryn. Why the fuck he has to be everywhere my sister is, I don't have a fucking clue. But it's fucking annoying. Vinny and Jonah are seated next to them.

I nod as I pass, pick Graycee up, and take her spot beside her mother, and set her on the other side of me. Then I grab Kathryn's hand and squeeze it. I can see the tears falling down her face, and I fucking hate it. I know I'm an asshole. One minute, I'm a straight-up prick, kicking her out of my bed when I'm done with her. And the next, I want to comfort her and wipe those fucking tears away.

Trust me. I don't get it either. It is what it is, though. Never said I could explain it.

Throughout the service, Kathryn continues to squeeze my hand. Her tears are silent. Almost like she's practiced crying without making a sound.

When we get home a few hours later, I take Graycee into the games room and turn the television on for her. Aliyah and Liam aren't far behind me.

"Can you watch her for a bit?" I ask my sister.

"Of course. But first, give me your credit card. We're doing some online shopping. Your daughter needs new clothes." Aliyah holds out a palm to me, her eyes expectant.

I draw my wallet from my pocket, pull out my AMEX, and hand it over to my sister. "She's five, Aliyah. She doesn't need Versace," I remind her.

Aliyah gasps, like I've offended her or something. "Ah, yes, she does! Don't worry, Gray. I'm going to teach that little girl how to be stylish *and* spend your money while doing it." She laughs.

"I don't care how much money she spends, Lia. I just don't think she needs to be running around in two-thousand dollar dresses she's gonna grow out of in a week." I shake my head before walking out of the room and making my way upstairs in search of Kathryn.

Chapter Twenty-Two

Kathryn

I unzip my dress, letting it fall to the floor before reaching behind my back to unclasp my bra, and watch it do the same. I step out of the pooling material and walk into the bathroom. I feel like I need to wash this day away. Off me. Turning on the shower, I wait for the water to warm up, then slide my panties off and step under the hot stream.

Tipping my head back, I let the heat wash over me. If only it could wash away my pain too. I knew today would be hard. I don't know what I expected. I guess I just didn't expect it to be as difficult as it was. I'm thankful I had Gray there.

The comfort I took from him, just having him holding my hand, keeping me grounded... I don't think he'll ever know how much it means to me that he did that. He didn't have to be there for me.

Is it possible that he could ever forgive me for what I did? That ember of hope ignites within me again at the thought.

I doubt it. I sit down under the water and bring my knees up to my chest. My forehead falls forward against my thighs and the tears don't just fall. They pour out of me like a tsunami. A wave of anguish like I've never felt before takes over my body. My chest heaves with my sobs. I'm so lost right now. I have no idea what I'm supposed to do. I just need to know what to do. I need Grayson to hate me. I need him to stop giving me so many mixed signals.

"Kathryn, come on." The water shuts off and then a pair of familiar hands reaches in and lifts me to my feet.

Kylie Kent

"Why are you here?"

"Because you need me," Grayson says.

"You hate me. You don't care about me. Why are you here? Just leave me alone." I push against his chest. I'm not really mad at him. I'm mad at myself. But right now, it's easier to lash out at him.

"Don't you think I would if I could? I can't fucking stay away from you, Kathryn. You're right. There are times when I do hate you. I hate what you did. But I can't stop fucking loving you either. Trust me, I've tried." He sighs, heavy and deep in his chest, before wrapping a towel around my body.

"No, you don't love me. You need to hate me, Gray. It's easier if you hate me. I left you, remember? I broke us. Just hate me, damn it." My hands ball into fists as I slam them against his chest.

He grabs my wrists to stop me. "It's okay. Kathryn, it's going to be okay." Then he tugs me close to his body, dropping my arms as he holds me tight to his chest. "It's going to be okay," he repeats.

"It's not okay, Gray. They're going to find me here, and you're the one who will pay the price. What if they find Graycee? What if they go after her for what I did?"

"Who? Kathryn, who the fuck are you talking about? I'm fucking tired of all the games, the

226

secrecy. Enough already. Just fucking tell me who it is."

"All of them. The cops, the Duvals, and God only knows who else," I choke out, close my eyes, and wait for the other shoe to drop.

Gray's fingers dig into my arms. He pulls my body back to look me in the face. "What?"

I shake my head and peer up at him. I shouldn't have told him. I knew I shouldn't. "Nothing. I didn't say anything. I'm fine. Just... I'm fine." I try to get out of his hold, but his grip only tightens.

"The cops? The Duvals? What the fuck happened, Kathryn?"

I shake my head, over and over again this time, as the tears fall down my face. I'm surprised I have any left to cry. "Gray, you have to leave it alone. I didn't sacrifice everything... I didn't destroy us for this to hurt you now. I can't... I can't let them get to you."

"For fuck's sake, Kathryn, no one is going to get to me. I'm fine. I'm right here." He picks me up and walks out of the bathroom.

Then Gray carries me into his bedroom. If I had the energy, I'd fight him. But I don't. I'm drained, emotionally and physically. He sits down on the little sofa against the far wall with me on his lap.

"Please, just tell me what happened. Whatever it

is, I can fix it. You have to tell me. If the Duvals are involved... You have no idea what that family is capable of, Kathryn. What they'd do to Graycee to get to you if that's what they wanted. You have to tell me. Everything," he says.

"I..." I open my mouth and then stop, close my eyes again, and inhale a breath. He's right. I need to figure out how to protect Graycee, how to protect Gray, and it's pretty freaking evident that I can't do either of those things on my own. I blink my lashes open. "I never got a scholarship like I told you, to go to school. I... I paid for college by hacking into bank accounts and making small withdrawals. Usually no one would notice, just small amounts here and there."

"You hacked into bank accounts? How do you even know how to do that?"

"My father taught me, when I was younger." I shrug. "I thought if I only took the money from those who earned it through illegal means, then I wasn't really doing anything wrong. It's not like I was stealing from hardworking, honest people."

"You stole money from crime families?" he asks.

I nod, and his body stiffens beneath me.

"My family? Liliana's?"

"No, never."

"Okay, so you stole money from the Duvals. That's why you think they're looking for you?"

"I don't think, Grayson. I know they are."

"How?"

"The day I left..." I stop speaking when I see the hurt in his eyes before forcing myself to continue. "I went for a run. That's all. I left you sleeping and went out for a jog that morning," I tell him. "I was approached by two men. Detectives. They hand-cuffed me and took me to the police station."

"What the fuck? Why didn't you tell me?" he asks.

"I couldn't. They... they wanted me to testify," I admit for the first time to anyone.

"Testify about what?"

"Against you." I close my eyes. I just need to get it all out. "They showed me pictures... bodies... They said they knew you and your brother had done it. Killed those men. And they wanted me to testify against you. They said if I told the court that you confessed to the murders, then they wouldn't turn me over to the Duvals. They had pages of transfers... said they had proof that linked the withdrawals to me. I never told anyone what I was doing, Grayson. But somehow they knew. I messed up somewhere and left a trace. Then they showed me what would happen to me if I didn't comply, if the Duvals got their hands on me." I push out the breath I didn't know I was holding and open my eyes.

Gray is staring at me. Just staring. Silent and not blinking. "I didn't kill anyone, Kathryn," he finally says after a long pause.

"I know that. I never thought you did," I tell him. "I didn't know what to do. I couldn't testify against you, Grayson. I wouldn't. But I also didn't want them to give me to that family. I got scared. So I ran."

"You should have told me. You should have come to me. We could have fixed it."

"Don't you get it? I left to protect you. If I wasn't here, they couldn't use me against you. I wasn't going to be the reason anything bad happened to you. If they turned me over to the Duvals, if those men knew I was with you, they would have come after you too. I didn't know what to do," I repeat. "I was trying to protect you."

"How much?" he asks.

"What?"

"How much did you steal from them?"

"Thirty grand. But the paperwork the detectives showed me... they made it look like I'd taken five hundred thousand," I say.

"I would have given you the money. For school.

If you told me you couldn't afford it, I would have given it to you."

"I know." I shake my head. "I didn't want your money. Your family's pity. I didn't want you to think I was with you to get something out of it. It sounds so stupid now. I know that. I thought I was careful. I thought I had it under control."

Gray pulls my head to his chest as his arms close around my back. "I thought you were dead. Then, when I saw you in that newspaper clipping, I thought that you just didn't love me like I love you. Because how could anyone leave someone they love without so much as a note? An explanation?" he says, his voice quiet.

"I love you, Grayson. I've always loved you. I never stopped loving you," I tell him. When he doesn't reply, I look up at him. "Say something. Yell at me, anything, just say something."

"I'm going to fix this. I won't let anything happen to you or Graycee."

"I can't let anything happen to you either." I hold back another sob.

Gray pulls his phone out of his pocket and stabs at the screen before he puts it to his ear. "Lia, I need you to have a sleepover with Graycee in the guest room."

I don't hear what his sister says. But then Gray's chest vibrates beneath me, his growl deep and unexpected. "Don't take her out of this fucking house, Aliyah. Use the guest room." He hangs up the phone without waiting for a response. "I need to talk to my dad... and Vinny."

"They're going to hate me even more than they do now." I shake my head, and Gray sighs.

"They don't hate you."

I give him that look, the one that says: *Are you serious right now?*

Grayson smirks. "Okay, maybe most of them do, but Vinny doesn't."

Chapter Twenty-Three

Grayson

I t's game day. And not just any game. *The fucking game*. The Stanley Cup Championship. That trophy is ours. I can feel it. This is the dream, something I've wanted my entire life. Kathryn and Graycee are watching from the family box, and having them here with me is everything.

I've always wanted this trophy, but knowing my daughter is watching makes me want to win even more, fight even harder for that Cup. Coach has been going on and on, talking plays and strategies. I've listened to most of it. None of its new information. We just need to go out there and play hard.

"Okay, let's go. You guys are ready for this. This is your night," Coach says.

I'm pumped walking down the tunnel. The Castle is the loudest I've ever heard it tonight. We head out to the ice. I have King on one side of me and Luke on the other as we stand and listen to the national anthem.

When the song finishes, I look from my left to my right. "You good?" I ask King. The fucker seems off. Could just be nerves though.

"Great," he grunts and skates over to the puck drop, which he loses. The wingers have it now and they're not about to give it up so easy.

By the end of the second period, we're tied. Everyone is exhausted.

I sit on the bench in the locker room and tug my jersey over my head. One of the PT guys walks over and starts working at my shoulders. I shake him off. I don't need that shit. What I *do* need to do is to call my daughter. Hear her voice.

I pick up my phone and dial Vinny's number. He's sitting with Kathryn and Graycee.

"Gray, you should be getting ready for the next period, not calling me," he says.

"Fuck off, and put my daughter on the phone," I tell him.

"Daddy, you're so close to winning." Graycee's voice flitters through the speaker and I smile.

"Yeah, I am. Are you having fun?" I ask her.

"So much fun. Uncle Vinny got me a hot dog and chocolate milk," she says.

"That's good. Put Uncle Vinny back on, baby." I wait for her to pass the phone over to my brother.

"Yeah?" Vinny asks.

"Bring Kathryn and Graycee down to the bench five minutes out. I want them there when we win," I tell him.

"Will do. Now go and do whatever it is you all do during breaks and then go back out there and fucking win that trophy. I don't want to hear the old man's shit if you don't win," Vinny grunts.

"You and me both." I cut the call and throw my phone on the towel beside me. Then I wave my hand at the PT fucker, and he comes back over.

Before I know it, it's third period. I look at the clock. We have five minutes left, and Kathryn and

Graycee are standing just behind the bench. Luke, King, and I rush the crease. I pass the puck to King and watch in dismay as it flies right over the fucking net, rebounding off the plexiglass.

I check Liam into the boards as I fight to get to the puck. "What the fuck is your problem?" I ask him.

He doesn't say anything, just looks up to the box where my sister is seated before determination darkens his features. About fucking time too. The guy needs to get his head out of his ass and fucking play to win. Those numbers on the clock are taunting me as I watch the seconds slip away like sand in an hourglass. I do not want this to go into overtime. I want that Cup already.

King has the puck again. He slaps it to Luke, but misses the fucking pass. It bounces off one of the Nashville wingers' skate and the fucker shoots down the ice. I take off after him. I don't know if I've ever skated this fast in my life. I'm pushing myself, my muscles burning, but I can't feel anything but the chill of the breeze across my face. I manage to steal the puck, and by some miracle, break away back towards our net.

King calls out. He's open. He's ready to score. But something in my gut tells me to go for it myself.

So I do. I take the shot and watch. And it's like everything happens in slow motion as the puck soars over the blocker side of Nashville's goalie. The horns sound out, the crowd fucking erupts, and it sinks in.

We did it. We actually fucking did it. We won.

And then King curses under his breath before I watch him rush over to the bench and jump over the boards. Then the fucker disappears down the tunnel while the rest of the team jumps on top of me. I push them off and skate over to where Graycee is bouncing up and down. Kathryn is smiling so fucking wide, and it occurs to me that I haven't seen her smile like this since our college days.

I reach down, scoop my daughter up, and then wrap an arm around her mother's back and pull her into me, the bench wall still separating us. My lips slam onto Kathryn's and my tongue delves into her mouth.

"Congratulations, you did it." She smiles at me when I pull away again.

"Thank you," I tell her.

"You want to do a victory lap with me, baby?" I ask Graycee.

"Really? I can?" she asks.

"Of course you can. This is your castle, remember?"

I don't think anything could have prepared me for this feeling. I'm fucking elated over our win, over having my daughter in my arms as I skate a victory lap. It's the best thing in the fucking world. Until my father and brother wave me over from where they're standing on each side of Kathryn with matching somber expressions on their faces. Certainly not the look a team owner should have after his guys just won the Stanley Cup.

"What's up?" I ask them.

"We have to leave. Now," Dad says.

"What? We just won—"

"Cover her ears." He cuts me off and points to Graycee.

I hand her over to Kathryn, reach up, and place my palms over each side of Graycee's head. Then I wait for my Pops to say whatever the fuck it is he's pissed about now.

"King was just shot, out in the parking lot, right in front of your sister. Let's go."

I drop my hands, jump over the bench, take hold of Kathryn's arm, and tug her and Graycee towards the locker room. I look from my dad to my brother. "What the fuck happened?"

"I'll fill you in on the way. Vinny's going to take the girls home," Dad says.

"Daddy? What's wrong?" Graycee asks me while I frantically yank at my laces.

"Nothing, baby. I just have to go help Poppy with something. You go with your mama and uncle, and I'll be home as soon as I can, okay?" I tell her.

"Okay, but we have cake. I made you a winner cake." She smiles as she peers up at me.

"And I can't wait to eat it." I chuck my skates across the room, pick up my bag, and kiss my daughter on her head. "Make sure they're safe," I tell Vinny.

"Always," he says.

The lot is taped off, onlookers and media outlets in every corner, while cops run around like ants under a magnifying glass. After tucking Graycee into my brother's car, I follow my dad to his and jump into the passenger seat.

"Okay, what the fuck is going on?" I ask as soon as we're pulling away from the chaos we left behind at The Castle.

"I've had threats. Against your sister. I was told to throw the game or risk losing her," he grunts.

"What the actual fuck? Why didn't I know about this?"

"I told King to throw the game, and he was doing a fucking good job at it too."

"Again, why the fuck didn't anyone tell me?" I snarl.

"I knew you'd go off half-cocked. I thought if we threw the game, I'd have more time to find the fucking assholes who were threatening me and put an end to them."

"Is Aliyah okay?" That should have been my first question.

"She just watched the man she loves get shot. So, no, your sister is not fucking okay. Physically, she's fine. King jumped in front of the bullet that was aimed at her," Dad says.

That fucker took a bullet meant for my sister? Fucking hell, I'm going to have to let the asshole marry her after all, aren't I?

"King? How bad is he?"

"I don't know yet."

When we get to the hospital, it's already a media circus. Reporters are everywhere, and I'm not helping the situation by walking through in my uniform, socks, an obvious lack of shoes. Pops pulls some strings and we are escorted back to Liam's room. I spot my sister and go straight for her.

"He's going to be okay, Lia," I say, wrapping an arm around her shoulders and pulling her against me.

"What if he's not? This is my fault. I never should have gotten him involved in our world," she sobs against my jersey. I can only imagine how I smell right now. But she doesn't seem to care.

"Like you could have stopped him. That stupid son of a bitch loves you. Fuck, he chose you over fucking hockey, Lia. If that's not love, I don't know what is," I tell her. "I just fucking wish someone would have let me in on what was fucking happening. I could have prevented all of this."

There's that feeling in my gut again. The one that comes and goes depending on the day. Whenever my rage gets the best of me or I can't see the shit that's right in front of my face. Whenever I'm getting close to Kathryn, only to pull away because I can't let go of the past. Can't figure out a way to forgive her. Whenever my daughter looks up at me and I see her mother staring back through eyes that are so much like mine.

Right, it's guilt. I recognize it now.

Not long after I walk into the room, Liam wakes up and asks my sister to marry him. I know they've been joking about it for weeks now, doing whatever they could to get under my skin. But, somehow, I don't think that's what's going on here. It's not the drugs talking either. He's fucking serious.

"King, you fucking asshole. You should have told me." I point at him.

"I told him not to," my father chimes in. "Liam, the doc says you're going to be fine. Just a couple of through-and-throughs. Lucky for you, the bastard missed anything vital."

"What about hockey?" My sister's voice is strained.

"Well, he's got a few months of recovery ahead of him before he gets back out on the ice again," Dad says. "But—"

Liam stops him short. "What's happening? Did you find him?" It's obvious he means the shooter.

"Vinny did." Dad nods, the glare he's aiming my way telling me not to press him for more when we're in mixed company. AKA Liam's family. He knows what I was going to ask. Vinny is supposed to be with Graycee, not running around on the streets.

I remind my father of as much as soon as we're making our way back down the hall.

"Your brother says the girls are safe at your house. But he's handling something. You know he wouldn't leave my granddaughter unprotected. Says he thinks the guy works for the Duvals. He did nothing to hide his face from the cameras," Dad tells me.

"The Duvals?" I ask.

"Yeah, why?"

Fuck! Kathryn.

"I gotta go." I rush out of the hospital doors, only to remember I didn't drive.

Lucky for me, Luke is walking in at the same time.

"I need your keys," I tell him. "I need to get home. Now."

He takes one look at me and nods. "Come on. I'll drive."

Chapter Twenty-Four

"Kathryn? Graycee?" Gray's voice echoes through the house.

"Daddy's home." Graycee jumps up off the sofa and runs out to the hallway. I follow her, catching up just as she throws herself into her father's arms.

"Hey, baby." He holds her tight to his chest and kisses her head, while I stand there in the foyer, not really sure what to do with myself. Gray's teammate is right behind him.

"Um, I can take her upstairs. She needs to get ready for bed," I tell Gray after another moment of awkward silence.

"Why?" he asks before turning on his shoeless feet to walk down the hall towards the games room with Graycee still in his arms.

"Grayson, you just won the Cup. You should be celebrating with the team," I call out as I trail behind them.

"Maybe, but I'm content to celebrate right here. With my favorite girl in the whole world," he says.

"Who's your favorite girl, Daddy?" Graycee asks him.

"You are, baby. Do you see any other girls around here?"

"Mama's a girl," Graycee says, sounding so very matter of fact for a five-year-old.

"She is, and she's my second favorite girl." Gray peers over one shoulder to smirk at me before setting our daughter down on her feet again. "Graycee, how about you go with Uncle Luke and get that cake I can't stop thinking about?"

She doesn't respond before running off towards the kitchen with *Uncle Luke* rushing after her. As soon as they disappear around the corner, Gray stalks over to me. His hand wraps around the back of my head and then his lips are on mine. I melt into him. Ever since I told him about the police, the Duvals, and the reason I left, a huge weight has been lifted off my shoulders and whatever wedge I put between us seems to have dissipated too.

He's still in his gear, his hair sweat-drenched and sticking to his forehead. "Mmm, you should shower," I tell him.

"Are you saying I stink?" He laughs.

"Yes, I am." I scrunch up my nose.

"A shower sounds like a great idea. You should join me." He nods like it's a done deal before reaching down and grabbing my hand.

"I'm not leaving Graycee with Luke to go shower with you, Grayson."

"Yeah, probably not the best idea. Who knows what the fucker'd teach her?" Gray leans in and kisses my forehead. "I'm really fucking glad you were there tonight."

"Me too," I tell him.

"I'll be right back. Save me some cake. Don't let

Luke eat it all," he says before running out of the room.

I head into the kitchen to find my daughter. Luke is already handing her some paper plates, with the dessert tray in one hand. "You take these. I'll take the cake," he tells her.

"Okay. Do you think my daddy will like it?" Graycee asks him.

"Are you kidding me? He's going to love it. He's going to eat so much of this cake there'll barely be any left for the rest of us."

I smile. Everyone in Gray's life has taken to Graycee so well. When Luke notices me watching them, he stiffens and his easygoing features harden. He's never been outright rude or disrespectful to me, but I get that feeling he's only being polite on the surface.

"I can take that," I offer. "Gray's just run up for a shower."

"I've got it." Luke walks past me and heads back into the games room.

"Here, I'll take the plates. Why don't you run upstairs and get that drawing you did for Daddy," I tell Graycee.

Her eyes widen. "I almost forgot!" she squeals as she sprints off down the hall.

I make my way to the games room in tense silence with Luke in tow. He sets the cake up on the bar so I set the plates down next to it. "You played really great tonight," I say in a weak attempt at making small talk.

"I'm in the NHL. I play great every game," he says.

"Okay then." I cross the room and start picking up some of the toys Graycee left strewn about while we were waiting, smiling to myself as my eyes flick around the space.

It's funny. When we first arrived, this was the ultimate bachelor pad. Now, it looks like a kid's play-room. Full of toys, dollhouses, everything a little girl could possibly want.

I can still feel Luke's glare, and when I turn around, I see him leaning against the bar with his arms folded over his chest.

"Is it me or do you just hate the world?" I ask him.

"It's just you," he says.

"Well, at least you're honest."

"More than I can say for some of us," he sneers. "What are your plans here, Kathryn? Playing house with Gray? You trying to get your claws back into his heart so you can rip it out for good the next time you decide to take off? Or you just looking for a cash cow, a former puck bunny hoping for the next big score?"

"I didn't mean to hurt him."

"You left of your own free will. What did you think would happen? You knew exactly what you were doing and you knew it would hurt him. So, yeah, you definitely meant it," Luke says.

"Okay, I... I'm not going to try to change your mind about me. What you think about me doesn't matter. I had reasons for doing what I did, and Gray knows them. Whatever happens between us now is just that, between us, and not anyone else," I tell Luke.

"Mama, I found it!" Graycee comes running back into the room, waving her picture around in one hand.

"That's great. I think Daddy's going to love it." I do my best to smile at her, though I can feel how strained it is.

"Can we have cake now?" she asks.

"We need to wait for Daddy. It's his cake, remember?"

"Well, Uncle Luke can share the cake. He won too," Graycee says.

"What's this I hear about you giving my cake

away, baby?" Grayson walks into the room, wearing a pair of grey sweats and a Knights t-shirt.

"Mama says it's nice to share," she tells him.

"Huh, guess it is, then." Gray picks Graycee up and sits her on top of the bar, next to the cake. "You made this?" he asks her.

Graycee's head bobs up and down. Truth is I made the cake and she helped. She did, however, do all the decorating on her own. The chocolate frosting is spread very unevenly around the top of the cake, and sprinkles of all kinds cover the surface.

"It's the best cake I've ever seen," Grayson says, and I take the opportunity to slink away.

I'll let him have this moment with his daughter and friend. I can't just sit in there while someone is hoping if they glare at me long enough I might just vanish. I call Liliana on my way upstairs.

"Hey you, congratulations," she says.

"For what?" I ask, and she sighs into the phone.

"For winning the game, duh."

"Oh, that was Gray, not me."

"Still, I bet you're all on cloud nine."

"You'd think so." I flop onto the bed with a humorless chuckle.

"What's wrong?" Liliana sounds like she's on high

alert now, like she's ready to jump through the phone and help me bury a body again. She's always been that friend. I just wish I could be the same for her.

"Do you think people can ever really move on from their past sins?" I ask her.

"Sins?" she parrots. "You getting your church on, Kathryn?"

"No, I mean, like, do you think I'll ever really be forgiven? For what I did to Grayson."

"First of all, you didn't just do that to Grayson," she says.

"I know. I'm sorry. I know my actions hurt you too, Lil."

"No—well, it did hurt me, but that's not what I meant. You hurt yourself, Kathryn. I think the question is do you forgive yourself?"

"No," I whisper. "I'm not sure I ever will."

"Have you thought about talking to someone? Like a professional? I know you don't want to tell me or anyone else why you left, but you could talk about it with a doctor."

"I told Gray," I admit.

"Oh... well... that's good. What'd he say?"

"Pretty much that I should have gone to him, and that he'll fix it."

"He'll fix it? What exactly does he have to fix?" Liliana asks.

"I... um... Okay, I'm going to tell you. But I want you to know, if you decide to not talk to me anymore afterwards, I get it. I understand, and I will always be grateful for you being in my life for how ever long I get to have you, Lil. Always."

"Kathryn, cut the bullshit. You know I'm your ride or die. So come on now. Out with it already," she says.

"I'm sorry. I just... I'm not proud of what I did. I was young and stupid," I tell her. "I stole money to pay for college. I used to hack into bank accounts, make withdrawals from crime families. Because I thought if I took it from them, it wasn't as bad as taking it from people who actually needed it."

"You stole money...? From crime families?" she asks, her words coming out slowly, deliberately.

"I did. But I never stole from your family, Lil. Or Gray's," I rush out.

She laughs. "It's funny you think you'd still be alive right now if you stole from my family."

"I'm sorry..."

"Kathryn, you were right."

I hold my breath. Because I know. I know this is where I lose her. I always knew it was going to happen, and I guess that was why I selfishly kept it from her, so I wouldn't. "I know," I say aloud.

"You were young and stupid. What the fuck were you thinking stealing from crime families? Do you have any idea what these people do to thieves?" she hisses through the phone.

"I know," I repeat. "I'm sorry."

"Who? What families? I'm guessing if you ran, it's because you got caught."

"I... I was taken in for questioning by two detectives. They gave me a choice: either testify against the Monroes, against Grayson, or they'd turn me over to the Duvals. They had papers that made it look like I took a lot of money. I didn't. I mean, I took some, but not as much as they were trying to say."

"Gray was right. You should have told him. What could they possibly have on him? He's as clean as a whistle," Liliana says.

"They had a whole damn folder, graphic pictures of bodies, murders they claimed he committed with the help of his brothers and father."

"I doubt that Grayson had anything to do with that." She sighs. "Okay, I'm coming back to Vancouver. I'm not about to leave you out there and wait for the wolves to find you."

"No, you don't have to do that. I'm okay. Really."

"Too bad. I just messaged the pilot. The jet'll be ready in two hours."

"I love you, Lil."

"I love you too, Kathryn." She disconnects the call, and I look up at the ceiling.

Liliana made a valid point. *Can Gray ever really forgive me if I can't even forgive myself?*

Chapter Twenty-Five

Grayson

"**O**kay, I think it's way, way past your bedtime, sweetheart, and Uncle Luke has a party to get to," I tell Graycee before picking her up off the bar.

"I like parties," she says with a hopeful look in her eyes. I swear they can even sparkle on command.

"I bet you do, and when it's your birthday, we can throw a really big one."

"Can my party be at The Castle?"

"It can be anywhere you want it to be. Now, come on. Say goodbye to Uncle Luke."

"Bye, Uncle Luke!" she sings.

"Bye, Graycee girl. See you later." Luke follows us out of the games room. He walks towards the front door while I head upstairs.

I ate that cake and got Luke out of here as quickly as I could without seeming rude. After I watched Kathryn sneak off, it took everything in my power to keep from going after her. But I didn't want to disappoint my daughter.

I find Kathryn in Graycee's room. Tonight, I think I'm going to make her come to my bed, where she should be. Should have always been.

I walk into the closet and find Graycee a pair of pajamas. "Here, baby, go get ready for bed. And don't forget to brush that chocolate off your teeth," I say while holding open the bathroom door.

Graycee slams it behind her because, in her words, *girls need privacy*. Kathryn told me she's been teaching our daughter about privacy and how her body is hers. It's not something that would have occurred to me to teach a five-year-old. But Kathryn is a great mom.

"Hey, you missed out on some really good cake," I tell her.

"I'm watching my weight." She shrugs.

"Why would you do that? Your body is amazing. You don't need to watch it. Better yet, I'll watch it for you, seeing as I seem to appreciate the view far more than you do." I sit next to Kathryn on the bed.

"That's 'cause you're a perv." She smirks, peering up at me as a few loose strands of blonde hair fall over her eyes.

"Only when it comes to you." I lean down, my hands landing on each side of her head. "We're gonna get Graycee to sleep, and then I'm taking you to my bed."

"I should stay with her."

"Kathryn..." I wait for her to look at me again. "I wasn't asking."

She rolls those blue eyes of hers and the bathroom door opens.

It doesn't take long for Graycee to pass out, her mouth gaping open like a fish out of water as the room fills with the sounds of her small snores. She didn't even last one story. I pluck the book out of Kathryn's hand, pull her up off the bed, and drag her to my bedroom, where I leave the door open just slightly, in case Graycee wakes up and wants to wander in.

"What's wrong?" I ask Kathryn. "Why didn't you stick around for cake?"

"I called Lil. I told her. Why I left." That's not what I asked, but it is something.

"What she say?"

"That you were right." Kathryn sighs.

"I'm always right," I remind her.

"She's coming back to Vancouver."

"I bet she is." I know Liliana, which means I also know that she won't be coming alone. Her father is the new reigning Don after all. Besides being fucking ruthless, Theo Valentino just so happens to be wrapped around his daughter's finger. Anything that girl wants, she gets.

"When did Vinny head out?" I ask Kathryn as I pick up my phone to call my brother, ready to let him know exactly what I think about him leaving my girls alone when I specifically asked him to keep an eye on them.

"He didn't. He went downstairs, to the basement. Told me to keep Graycee in the games room until you got home," Kathryn says.

"He's in the basement? Here?" I repeat, dropping my phone on the bed and jumping to my feet before I realize what I'm doing.

"Well, that's what he said. I didn't watch him go. Why?"

"No reason. Stay here. I'll be back." I don't wait around for her to respond. Instead, I take the stairs two at a time and rush to the basement.

I should have known whatever Vinny was doing down here wasn't something I really wanted any part of. I know my brother. I know what he does for my father, what I've managed not to do, so far.

"What the fuck? My daughter is upstairs asleep," I growl.

Vinny turns to look at me. There are four other guys in the room, friends of my brother, employees of my father. "Go back upstairs, Gray," he tells me.

"Why is he here?" I point to the guy hanging from the chains that are currently attached to the rafters. I don't know who the fuck he is, but he looks like he's seen better days.

"The boys caught him trying to break in through the side door," Vinny tells me.

"Break in? Here?" I point to the ground, as if to clarify he means my fucking house. Someone tried to fucking break into my fucking house while my daughter was here. While Kathryn was here. While I wasn't.

"Yep," Vinny pops his P.

"Why?" I ask.

"No idea. Fucker's not talking." Vinny tilts his head at me with a sinister smirk on his lips. "You wanna try to get him to talk?"

I look from my brother to his hostage. The thought that this fucker was here to potentially harm my daughter or Kathryn makes my blood boil. Fuck yes, I want to find out why. I look to the tools Vinny has lined up on the floor. Devices to inflict pain, implements of torture.

"I'll be right back." I look back up to Vinny. "And, yeah, I think I do want to give it a go."

I run upstairs and quickly find a hockey stick and a bag of pucks. If you've ever had one of those little black disks come flying at you full force, you'd know it hurts like a motherfucker. I don't need my brother's little tool bag. I have my own.

The moment I rush back down the steps, Vinny looks my way and eyes my gear with a cocked brow. I ignore him, dump the pucks onto the ground, and walk right up to the guy hanging from the chains.

"I'm only going to give you one chance. Why the fuck are you here?" I ask him. The asshole smiles at me and spits blood in my direction. I step back to avoid the splatter. "Don't say I didn't warn you." Then I line up my first shot. "Ever been hit by a hockey puck?" I watch his glare bounce between me and the disk on the floor before a flicker of unease crosses his face. "No?" I raise a brow, matching Vinny's expression, as I dribble the puck and look the fucker dead in the eye. "That's okay. It only hurts a little."

I snap my stick back, bringing it off the ground and landing a perfect shot. The puck flies forward and hits him square in the temple when the fucker flinches and turns his head at the last minute. He screams out in pain. I'm pretty sure that blow was enough to shatter or at the very least splinter some bones. I line up my next shot and swing, this time aiming for his torso, and hit him right in the gut. A huge red welt forms instantly.

"Why are you here?" I ask him again.

"F-fuck you," he sneers at me, so I aim for his cock and hit my intended target.

"Why are you here?" I yell out over the sounds of his screams as I dribble the next puck in front of him.

"Her. I'm here for the woman and girl," he groans while attempting to press his thighs together and relieve some of the sting. "I'm just doing my job, man."

I don't know what comes over me. But I see red. Figuratively and literally. As I shoot puck after puck into his body, rage coursing through my own blood the more I spill *his*. "Why?" I yell out.

"I don't know. It... ah... Fuck! Stop!"

"Why the fuck are you here for them?" I'm screaming so loud my throat hurts and I can feel the veins in my forehead pounding.

"Boss w-wants them," he says.

"Who's your boss?" I lower my stick and pin the fucker with my glare. He's beaten, bloodied, bones broken. But none of it is enough to feed the anger still boiling in my veins.

"David Duval," he says. "Please let me go. I'll leave town. I won't come back. I swear. Just let me go," he pleads.

My stick smacks against the ground. I don't even remember dropping it as I walk over to Vinny's little tool bag and pick up a knife. "You see, the problem I have with that is that you were here for my daughter," I grind out. The guy shakes his head as I grab a fistful of his hair in my left hand. "I can't let you breathe the same air as her. Any asshole willing to hurt a little girl doesn't deserve mercy," I tell him before jamming the sharp end of the blade into the side of his neck.

When I pull it out again, blood is flowing out of the gaping hole like a river. I stand there and watch, not caring that I look like I just stepped out of a horror movie. I'm too hypnotized by the sight. By all the red.

"Fuck. Grayson." Vinny grabs my hand, takes the knife, and tosses it to the floor. "Clean this mess up," he barks out to the other four guys in the room. Then turns back to me. "Come on." He takes hold of my arm and drags me up the stairs. "You didn't have to do that. I would have finished it."

"It's fine," I grunt.

"No, it's not fine. You're a fucking hockey player, Grayson, not a killer." Vinny shoves me into the guest bathroom.

"He was after my daughter, Vinny. What the fuck did you expect me to do?" I push at his chest, sending him back a few steps. Away from me and my rage.

"Get in the shower. And give me your clothes. I need to burn them."

I grab the collar of my shirt and pull it over my head before tossing it to the floor.

"Why do you think the Duvals are after Kathryn?"

"She stole from them," I tell him. "Six years ago. That's why she ran. She told me she was approached by two cops who showed her photos of some bodies—bodies they claimed Dad, you, and me were responsible for putting in the ground. Then they gave her a choice between testifying against me or getting handed over to the Duvals."

"What the fuck did she steal from them?" he asks.

"Cash. She hacked into their bank accounts to pay for college."

"So she ran because she didn't want to testify against you but also didn't want to be handed over to the Duvals?"

"Yep."

"Huh, I knew there was a good reason," Vinny says.

"How'd you know? From the jump, you were the one insisting there was more to the story than what we knew."

"That woman loves you, Gray. That much is as clear as the grass is green. She wouldn't have just left without a good fucking reason." He sighs, and something flickers in my chest. Something both familiar and foreign.

She loves me?

I've wondered... I've been so fucking angry, because no matter how much I wanted to hate her, the love I have for her always outweighs it.

"She also told Graycee about you. That's not what women do when they *want* to keep their kid away from the father," Vinny says.

I step into the shower, dipping my head as I watch the water turn red before running down the drain.

"This isn't over, Gray. Duval won't give up that easily," my brother repeats what I'm already thinking.

"I know."

Chapter Twenty-Six

Kathryn

The mattress dips and my lashes flutter open to Gray's deep-green eyes. "Sorry... I drifted off."

"It's okay. Jump up," he says.

I climb off the bed, ready to go back to the room I share with Graycee, when Grayson pulls the blankets back. His gaze rakes up and down my body. I might have helped myself to one of his Vancouver Knights t-shirts when he was gone.

"Don't even think of leaving this room, Kathryn. Get in." He nods to the bed.

"I should go check on Graycee." I pull at the hem of the shirt, attempting to cover more of my legs. Somehow I always feel naked around this man, no matter how much clothes I'm wearing.

"I just did. She's fine. Get in the bed, Kathryn. It's late," Gray says.

I walk over to the bed and climb in. He slides in next to me and covers us both with the blanket. Then he reaches over and tugs on the chain of the bedside lamp, and the room falls into darkness. I jump when I feel his palm land on the small of my back, and he pulls me closer to him. Once he's satisfied with where my body is positioned, his hand comes up and runs through my hair.

"I'm sorry," he says.

"Why are you sorry?"

"A lot of reasons. For a lot of things." Gray sighs. "I'm sorry for the way I've treated you the last few weeks. You didn't deserve that from me."

"I..."

"I'm not finished." He places a finger over my

lips. "I'm sorry that I didn't make you feel like you could have come to me for help back then. But, mostly, I'm fucking sorry that I gave up. That I accepted you were gone for good."

"It wasn't you, Grayson. I was scared. I was trying to do the right thing, to keep you safe," I tell him. "And what do you mean gave up?"

"I gave up on looking for you. I just stopped. I should have kept looking."

"You never would have found me. I made sure of it, Gray. There was nothing you could have done differently," I tell him.

"I still shouldn't have given up. I promise I will never give up on you again, Kathryn. I won't give up on us."

"Us? Do you really think we can be an *us* again...? After everything I've done?"

Grayson's fingers run up and down my cheek, ever so lightly. "I think we will always be an *us*, Kathryn. We probably have some shit to work through, but it's always been you. It will always be you."

I suck in a breath. I dreamed of this day, many times, but never in a million years did I expect it to happen. "I'm sorry that I left. I'm sorry that I didn't just come to you and tell you what happened. I'm sorry that I lied to you. I'm sorry that I stole that money. And I'm really sorry I kept Graycee from knowing you. I will never be able to make up for that, Gray. I know that, and I don't expect you to ever forgive me. I won't forgive myself."

Grayson wipes away the tear that slides down my cheek. "I will do everything I can to find a way to forgive you, Kathryn."

"It's okay."

Gray's breath touches my lips as he moves in closer. "I love you. With everything that's in me, I love you."

"I love you too," I whisper.

His lips press onto mine. Softly, so softly. Gray slides his tongue in to my mouth, and even his strokes are slow. Tender. He's not in a rush, and neither am I. His hand cups my cheek, his thumb rubbing delicate circles on my skin.

My leg hooks over his. The need to get closer to him never goes away. Gray rolls on top of me, covering my body with his as he settles between my legs. He props himself up with his left arm while his right explores my skin, maintaining the slow, tender pace of his kiss. I'm heating up until my moans are swallowed up by his mouth. I pull him close as my hips lift off the bed, seeking that friction my core so desperately needs.

Gray pushes up onto his knees. His heated gaze burns right through my skin, alighting every nerve ending I have in my body. He smiles at me. I haven't seen this smile in six years. It's the one he used to reserve just for me, when we were alone. He has a dimple on the right side of his face—it's always been one of my favorite features.

Scratch that. Everything about this man is my favorite. His body is larger than I remember it being in college, which I didn't think was possible. He was huge back then too. My hands travel over his shoulders, down his arms, and back up again. I move them along his chest and underneath his shirt. Gray reaches behind his neck and pulls the material off over his head. And my eyes can just make out the bruising on his torso. One of the downsides to hockey.

"Are you hurt?" I ask him.

"No. But I will be if I don't get inside you in the next sixty seconds," he says, pulling my underwear down my legs. Once they're off, he pushes my shirt—his Knights shirt—up and over my head. I lift off the bed to ease his efforts to undress me. "I forgot how much I like seeing you in my clothes," he says.

"I forgot how much I love wearing your clothes."

Gray removes his sweats and settles back between my thighs. He lines his cock up with my entrance. I'm ready for him. No prep work required here. He slowly slides his shaft inside me and lowers his upper body over mine. Maintaining eye contact, he brings his lips back to my mouth. His hand cups my cheeks and he starts moving. Back and forth. His pace slow. Torturously slow.

"I want this to last forever," he says against my lips.

"Mmm, me too," I tell him.

We continue making love, because this is not the kind of fucking we've always been good at. This is much more intimate than anything we've ever done before. Even back in college. I don't think we ever made love then either. We had sex, a lot of it, but this feels so different.

"I want you to come with me. Together, Kathryn. Always together," Gray says.

He moves his hand between our bodies, his thumb finds my clit, and he starts rubbing. Gray's mouth trails over to my neck. He bites down onto the soft skin near my shoulder, and my orgasm hits me like a lightning bolt. Shots of pleasure explode through my body, and Gray's movements become rigid as his cum coats the inside of my walls. He collapses on top of me before rolling to the side and wrapping an arm around my shoulders.

"That was..."

"Perfect," he finishes my sentence for me.

"Yeah, it was." I kiss his chest.

"Mama, Mama, wake up. Breakfast is ready! Uncle Vinny made me chocolate pancakes. Come on, Mama." Graycee is jumping on the bed and shaking me awake.

I peek one eye open. "I'm up," I say, grabbing her and pulling her down on top of me. "But first, I need snuggles." I pepper her face with kisses.

"But, Mama, pancakes," she whines. "Daddy says you have to get up and come eat."

"I don't recall saying that, princess," Grayson

chimes in. I look up, over the top of Graycee, and see him walking into the room. He reaches the edge of the bed and plucks her off me. "Why don't you run down and tell Uncle Vinny you can have one pancake while you wait for Mama to get dressed?"

"Okay." Graycee wiggles out of his arms and runs from the room while yelling out, "Uncle Vinny!" Mornings used to be a struggle. Now, my daughter can't wait to get out of bed and captivate her adoring audience.

"Why do I feel like second place to a plate full of pancakes?" Gray asks, watching Graycee's back speed off down the hall.

"Because you are." I laugh. "We all are."

Grayson pulls the blankets back. I'm still completely naked. Which I'm guessing he already knew. "Fuck, Kathryn, maybe they won't notice if we skip breakfast," he says while eyeing every inch of my skin.

I slide off the bed and run into the bathroom. "Actually, I'm starving," I call out behind me and slam the door in his face. After freshening up, I pick up a towel and wrap it around my upper body. When I walk out again, Grayson frowns.

"I'm going to burn all the towels. We should just

become a naked family," he says, and the expression on his face has him appearing far too serious.

"You know, you have a lot of great ideas. *That* is not one of them, though." I smile at him. "I'm going to get dressed real quick. You do not want to keep Graycee waiting for too long. Trust me, she looks sweet and innocent but that girl can throw down as fiercely as any hockey player. As fiercely as you, Grayson," I tell him.

His frown morphs into a smile. "Can't wait to see that," he says.

"You will regret those words, Grayson Monroe," I tell him before walking into Graycee's room. It's where I've been keeping all of my things.

Gray is not far behind me. "We should move your stuff into my closet. You know, make it *our* closet," he says.

My hands pause on the sweater I was grabbing down from a hanger. I turn to look at him. "Seriously? You want to share a closet with me?"

"I want to share everything with you, Kathryn."

I don't know what to say. I mean, I want that, more than I would like to admit, but I'm scared.

"If I say yes, is this where you laugh in my face, tell me how much you hate me and how that will never happen?" I blurt out without intending to verbalize my inner thoughts. My very real fears.

"That's not going to happen. You can say no, but I'll just move your stuff anyway." He walks into the closet and wraps his arms around my waist. "I'm sorry I was a jerk." His lips press against the top of my head.

"I deserved it. I know that, but... I just have insecurities. Which is not your fault. It's mine."

"I'm in this, Kathryn. One hundred percent. This isn't me setting you up for heartbreak. I never want to see you hurt. This is me finally getting what I've been waiting for, for a very long time," he says, "while hoping it's what you've been waiting for too."

Chapter Twenty-Seven

Grayson

It's day one after winning the Cup. I should be floating on cloud nine. Soaking in the win I've been gunning for since I could stay upright on a pair of skates. Instead, I'm sitting in the living room with my brothers and father, discussing family business. And I don't mean hockey.

I've filled my father in on the reason Kathryn left, the Duvals being after her and now Graycee too. He wasn't exactly thrilled to find out my girlfriend was lifting money from crime families. I haven't asked her to make a list of names. Though I should. To make sure we know how deep this goes, how many people might be out there looking for her.

Vinny told Dad about the guy who broke in last night, or attempted to break in at least. He also let our old man know that it was me who dealt with the fucker and not him. My father eyed me with a strange expression on his face, a mixture of pride and sorrow. It's not like I've never done anything for him before, but I usually try to keep my image clean. It's best for the team that way.

"Okay, we need to find out the names of the detectives who questioned Kathryn back then. And what the fuck they were trying to pin on us. Whatever it was, it sure as fuck didn't stick, or we would have heard about it by now," Dad says.

"What about Aliyah?" I ask.

"What about her?" he growls.

"They were threatening her, the Duvals. Why? They were blackmailing you to throw the game. That's not connected to Kathryn, not any way I can see," I tell him.

"My guess? Money. Simple as that. They threatened the one thing they knew could have me caving to their demands. The fuckers are always after lining their pockets the quickest and easiest way they can. The Championship landing on their doorstep was their golden ticket to using our name against us."

Vinny and I share a look. "Good to know the rest of us would be fed to the wolves in a ransom demand." My brother laughs.

"You three can protect yourselves." Dad points to me, then Vinny and Jonah. "Your sister can't."

Speaking of...

"Have you heard anything about King?" I ask.

"He's fine. He'll be in the hospital for a few more days. The docs have told him to take it easy," Dad says.

"Good thing it's off season then," I grunt. "Gotta say... this is not how I pictured spending it, by the way."

"You have a few months of downtime. Spend it with Graycee. Enjoy it. Because when you're back, we're going to have to fight like hell to keep that Cup."

"I want to take her to Disney," I say.

"Can I come? I've never been to Disney." Jonah shoots our father a look.

"No," I tell him.

"What? Why not?" he whines.

"Because Graycee is my daughter, and you're not. I'm not taking you to fucking Disney World, Jonah. You're a grown-ass man. Take yourself."

"Fine. I'll just go make my own kid so I have a reason to go to Disney then." He grins like he's clever or some shit.

"Spare us—and the rest of the world—the idea of you spawning children." Vinny chuckles, and Jonah flips him the bird.

"Okay, enough. We need to figure this shit out. Until then, keep Graycee and Kathryn within arm's reach. Don't let them go out on their own unprotected," Dad says. "I've already placed some extra guys around the perimeter."

"Thank you. Don't worry. I don't plan on letting them go anywhere." I smirk. If I had it my way, those two wouldn't leave my side. Ever. For anything.

"What if it wasn't just money?" Vinny questions after a long stretch of silence.

"What do you mean?" Dad asks.

"Aliyah? What if them wanting you to throw the game wasn't just about money?"

"What else could it be?"

"Who the fuck knows? But do we know if they

lost? On that game? Were they even betting on it? I'll ask around and find out. Gray put that guy down last night before I could question him about it. We know he's the same guy who pulled the trigger on Liam. The dumb shit smiled at the cameras. And we know that he works for the Duvals. But we don't know why. That bullet wasn't meant for Liam. It was meant for Aliyah. They missed, which means they're not done with her yet," Vinny says. "They'll try again."

My blood goes cold at the thought. Fucking assholes. Targeting women is supposed to be off-limits. They have nothing to do with this world, even if they end up being casualties of the men in this war in the long run.

"Aliyah is safe. She's at the hospital with Liam. I have a lot of guys there with her," Dad says.

"About that... are we really just gonna sit back and let her marry that fuckwit?" I lean into the sofa cushions and cross my arms over my chest. I was still in shock after the shooting. But the more I think about King and my sister, the less I like the idea. Bullet or no bullet.

"Yes," Dad, Vinny, and Jonah all say at the same time.

"Seriously? Am I the only one who thinks she can do better?" I grunt.

"He took a fucking bullet for her, Grayson. What more proof do you need that he loves her? He was going to throw the game, end his entire career for your sister," Dad says.

"She's still too good for him," I grumble under my breath.

"Of course she is, but he's who she's chosen, and the bastard has proven himself more than enough to have my blessing." Dad gives me that look that says I won't be winning this argument.

"Fine," I huff. "I'll go along with this shit idea and play happy families with the prick. But know that I am most certainly *not* happy about it."

"We know. We *all* know," Vinny groans. "You've made that much very clear, more than once." Then the fucker grins. "While we're on the topic of family, I really fucking hope I live long enough to see Graycee grow up. To see her become a teenager. A young woman."

"What? Why would you say that? You planning on dying on me?" I ask him.

"Not planning on it. But it's a tough life. And I can't wait to see how you react to her dating is all." He laughs.

I blink at him. "She's not going to date. She's not gonna even want to date."

"Yeah, sure she's not," Jonah says.

"Fuck off, all of you. That's not even funny," I hiss just as the doorbell sounds out through the house.

"Expecting guests?" Dad asks me.

"Well, if they got past your security, it can't be the bogeyman, now can it?" I push to my feet and stomp out of the room.

However, as soon as I open the door, I eat my words. It seems I was wrong.

"Theo Valentino, did I miss the memo that announced you were visiting?" I ask the bogeyman himself.

"Where's Kathryn?" Liliana barges past her father and into the house.

"Please, come on in," I call after her, my voice dripping with sarcasm. "She's in the games room with Graycee."

Liliana takes off through my house as I turn back to her father, who is still on the other side of my front door. He's not alone though. No, he has his son and nephew with him too.

"Dad's in the living room," I tell Theo, Alessandro, and Enzo. The three men nod and follow me inside. I stop in front of my father and gesture over my shoulder. "Dad, you've got a visitor."

"Valentino, what are you doing in town?" My dad stands and shakes hands with Theo. They've been friends for as long as I can remember.

"Liliana has it in her head that the Duvals are after her best friend," he says. "Any truth to that rumor?"

"Yes," Dad says, then quickly adds, "We're handling it."

"What have they done? And why are they after her?" This question comes from Liliana's brother.

"Lil didn't tell you?" I raise a brow at Alessandro.

"No, she didn't."

"It's a long story, but Kathryn hacked into a few bank accounts back in our college days. The Duvals were one of them," I explain as simply as I can.

"She hacked? You mean she stole money," Alessandro asks.

"Like I said, it's a long story."

"Okay, what are we doing to squash this threat?" Theo looks from me to my father expectantly.

"*We*?" Dad parrots.

"I didn't stutter when I said it. My daughter won't return home until she knows Kathryn is no longer in danger. Which means your problem just became my problem," Theo grunts, and Dad rakes an exasperated hand through his hair.

Sure, our families might be close. Friends and all. But things always get complicated when it comes to the Valentinos. The whole family is the *our way or no way* type.

"How about a drink?" Dad walks over to the liquor trolley and pours a hefty serving of amber liquid into several glasses.

"We found one of them last night, trying to break in here," Vinny chimes in.

"Where is he now?" Liliana's cousin asks.

"Gray put him down." Vinny smiles at Enzo. My brother looks like a proud parent bragging about their all-star kid.

I glare at him. Some things should be kept between us. In the family. "He was after my daughter," I say in way of explanation.

"I heard about that little... *development*. Congrats on becoming a girl dad," Theo says dryly. And something tells me he knows I'm in over my head here.

I smile anyway. "Thank you." I'm fucking proud of being a girl dad. I should get a shirt or something made. I pull out my phone and send Luke a message.

ME:

I need you to find me a shirt.

LUKE:

When did I become your personal assistant?

ME:

When you decided to become my #1 friend. Find me a shirt that says "proud girl dad" or some shit like that.

LUKE:

Seriously??? You're losing your cool factor.

ME:

I don't care.

LUKE:

Fine, but I'm gonna make sure it's pink too. Then I'm gonna take a pic and send it to the guys. So we can all share a laugh at your expense.

I ignore him, shove my phone back into my pocket, and return my focus to the group of men currently staring at me. "What?"

"Who you texting?" my dad asks.

"Luke. Why?"

"No reason." He shrugs.

"I heard Travis is a free agent and looking to get

transferred to the Knights," Alessandro says cooly, and you can almost hear a pin drop with the tension.

"Is he? I wouldn't know anything about that. We just won the Cup last night. Next season is next season's problem, for a few months anyway."

"You're not signing him. If the fucker moves here, my daughter will want to follow him, and I can't have that happening," Theo says in a way that tells the rest of us he isn't playing.

"Would you prefer another team sign him? Have Liliana move to a city where she doesn't know anyone at all?" Dad asks, and I know by my father's tone that he has every intention of acquiring the New York hotshot.

"What I'd prefer is for my daughter to drop his ass," Theo grunts.

"Well, as fun and informative as this has all been, I've got shit to do. Excuse me." I leave the room before someone can stop me and go in search of my daughter. It's my first day off and I'd much rather be spending it with her than anyone else.

Chapter Twenty-Eight

Kathryn

"**K**athryn, thank god!" Liliana rushes into the room and tackles me.

I'm sitting on the floor doing puzzles with Graycee—well, I was sitting. Now, I'm flat on my back with my best friend on top of me.

"Oh my god! You're going to squish me to death." I laugh.

"I was so worried," she says, climbing off me. "I... ah...I might have brought in the big guns."

"The big guns?" I ask her, my eyebrows shooting to my hairline.

"My dad's here, so are Alessandro and Enzo." She shrugs.

"You what? Why?"

"Because I'm not about to let anyone F-U-C-K with you," she says, censoring herself for Graycee's sake.

"That spells *fuck*," Graycee shouts proudly. Yes, my daughter can read. And spell apparently.

Liliana's jaw drops in shock as she gestures a thumb in Graycee's direction. "The kid knows how to spell?"

"Only some words," I say before looking to my daughter. "Graycee, Aunt Lil spelled a bad word, and we do not repeat bad words."

"It's okay. Uncle Vinny and Poppy say bad words all the time too," Graycee replies nonchalantly.

"So, Graycee, I heard you got to skate a victory lap last night at The Castle. Was it fun?" Lil asks while attempting to change the subject.

"Daddy took me around. My daddy won the Cup!" Graycee tells her.

"I know. How cool is that?" Liliana grins.

"It's cooler than the puck Uncle Liam gave me and that's really cool!"

"Huh, well, I brought you something *even* cooler from New York. I was walking past this shop the other day and saw these amazing dolls and dollhouses. Everything is being delivered tomorrow," Lil says, and Graycee's eyes widen.

"For me?" she asks.

"Yep, just for you."

"Thank you, Aunt Lil." Graycee jumps up and hugs Liliana.

I look at my best friend and my daughter, and I know that coming back here was a good thing. That Gray finding us was a good thing. Graycee's life is so much fuller now. She has so many people in her corner. It's not just us two anymore. She gets to grow up with a huge, extended family. Something I couldn't give her on my own.

"Daddy!" Graycee pushes back from Liliana and runs to Grayson when he walks into the room.

"Hey, baby, having fun?" he asks her.

"Did you go to work already?"

"I'm on vacation, baby. I'm all yours for the next few months," Gray says with a grin.

Graycee looks at him expectantly. "We're going to Disney now?"

"Not today, but soon. Promise." He kisses her head and sets her back down on her feet. Then he turns to Liliana. "Where are you all staying?"

"Dad got a house," she says while crossing her arms over her chest. "But I'm not leaving. What are we doing about this little problem?"

"You aren't doing anything about it. I'll have a room set up for you, on the other side of the house," Gray grunts.

I watch their interaction. They've always been friends. They knew each other long before I was ever in the picture. But something seems different about them now.

I push to my feet and walk over. "Lil, can you watch Graycee for five minutes? I'll be right back."

Then I take hold of Gray's hand and pull him out of the room, not waiting for Liliana's response. I tug him down the hall, look back over one shoulder, and then stop.

"Did you and Liliana ever have a thing?" I ask, keeping my voice down.

"A thing?" Gray repeats.

"You know, *a thing*?"

"I don't know? What's a thing, Kathryn?" He tilts his head and glares at me.

"Did you sleep with her? When I was gone? Did you guys have a thing? I mean, it's not a big deal. I wasn't here. You were free to do whatever and whomever you wanted. But I need to know... Did you? With Lil?"

Gray smirks. "You sound jealous, babe."

"I'm not jealous. More... curious?" I tell him. After all, I have no right to be jealous. Not after what I did to him.

"No. We did not have *a thing*. Nor would we ever." Grayson sighs.

"Okay. Sorry." I shake my head, trying to clear the image that thought put into my mind. "So why is there so much animosity between you two all of a sudden?"

"Because she helped you leave me. She knew, and she let me think you were fucking dead all these years, Kathryn."

"Okay." I don't know what else to say to that. "I get it. I do. But she was only looking out for me. If it helps, she was and has always been on Team Gray. She begged me not to leave you, Grayson. It was my fault I left, not hers."

"It doesn't help. But you're still fucking cute as hell when you're jealous." Gray wraps an arm around the back of my shoulders and pulls me up against his chest. Then he lowers his lips to my forehead.

"I wasn't jealous," I grumble against his shirt.

"Mmm, sure you weren't," he says, and his chest vibrates with a low chuckle. "Is it true? What you said before? About not being with anyone else...?"

"Yes." I lift my head and look him dead in the eye. "It was different for me, Gray. I knew where you were. Whereas you thought I was dead. You moved on. That's normal, and perfectly all right."

"I didn't fucking move on. Ever. But I wasn't celibate either," he says.

"I know. I've seen all the tabloids," I tell him. "It appears you have a thing for blondes."

"I have a thing for you. I was trying to find you in everyone I met..."

"I'm so sorry."

"It's okay. How about we grab Graycee and go make a pizza?" he suggests in a much lighter tone.

"Make a pizza?"

"Uh-huh, I'm officially on vacation and I can eat crap. So I want to eat crap and enjoy it." He grins.

"Okay, let's make the most fattening, crappy

pizza there is." I push up on my tiptoes, then quickly lower myself back down. I was about to kiss him before I second-guessed it.

Should I do that? Kiss him like I used to...

"Kathryn, kiss me," Gray says, clearly reading my mind. "If you want to kiss me, then fucking kiss me. Whenever, wherever, and in front of whomever."

I push back up and meld my lips with his, closing my eyes as I let myself sink into his embrace, into everything that is Grayson Monroe.

"Kathryn, can we have a chat?" Vinny comes into the kitchen with Jacob Monroe—the head of the Monroe family, AKA Gray's father—in tow. I came down to get Graycee a glass of water she insisted she needed before she'd go to sleep.

"Sure, what's up?" I ask, my eyes bouncing between the two very intimidating men.

"We need to know the names of the detectives who questioned you a few years back," Vinny says matter-of-factly. No question about it.

"It's been a long time. I don't remember what their names were," I tell him.

"Would you recognize 'em from a picture?" Jacob asks me.

"Probably." I close my eyes for a second. It's hard to forget the faces of the two people who derailed your entire life.

"Great. I'll grab a few photos for you to sift through then," Jacob says. "One more thing though, Kathryn."

I look up at him.

"If you break my son's heart again, it won't end so well for you. Mother of my grandchild or not."

I blink. Jacob Monroe just issued me a death threat. I'm not an idiot. I know what he's saying. And that he means every word. "I don't want to break his heart. But make no mistake, if I have to do something neither of us likes, to protect him, I will. Regardless of who my daughter's grandfather may be."

"Okay, well, how about we just agree that before

you do anything half-cocked, you're going to come to me first," Vinny chimes in with a smirk.

I nod my head while having no intention of doing that. If it comes down to me or Grayson, I will choose him. There isn't even a question about it.

I leave Vinny and Jacob in the kitchen, and just before I reach the stairs, Luke strolls in through the front door. Great, it must be my lucky night, having to deal with all the overprotective men in Grayson's life. All of whom aren't too keen on me, it seems.

"He's reading a book to Graycee. I'll let him know you're here," I say before pivoting on my heel, intending to walk away as quickly as I can.

"Kathryn?" Luke calls out. I stop and turn back to him. I only made it three steps. "I wanted to say I'm sorry. For what I said last night. I was an ass. And I'm sorry." He glances down, at the floor, then back up at me with a sheepish expression on his face.

"You were an ass, but I get it." I give him a polite smile—you know, the one you give when you don't really want to be smiling at someone—and rush up the stairs towards Graycee's room.

I stand in the doorway for a few moments and watch. Graycee's already knocked out but Grayson is still reading *Sleeping Beauty* to her.

"Luke's here," I tell him. "And she's asleep, so you can stop reading."

"Did you have any idea that all these fairy tales are aimed at women needing to find a man?" he asks me.

"Ah, yeah, it's kind of the point. Happily ever after."

"It's shit is what it is. We need books where the princess grows up to be independent, not wanting a fucking man." He rolls off the bed.

"Mmm, maybe you should write it. I'm sure it'd be a hit." I chuckle.

"I'll get rid of Luke. Meet me in our room, in our bed, naked." Grayson eyes me up and down and then walks out.

When did it go from his room, his bed, to ours?

Chapter Twenty-Nine

Grayson

I shouldn't be aroused right now. It probably should not turn me on so damn much that Kathryn is yelling at me, arguing with me. It does, though, and I feel like it's giving her an upper hand because my brain is hyperfocused on her body, on my dick wanting to get in *that* body.

"I'm not budging on this, Kathryn. It's not safe, and until we know that it is, she's not going." I cross my arms over my chest.

"It's illegal to keep a child home from school, Grayson. You can't keep her locked up in this house."

"Watch me." I raise an eyebrow. "And since when do you care about legalities? I'm pretty sure it's fucking illegal to hack into bank accounts."

"You know, I still know how to do that. I could bleed you dry within seconds, and you wouldn't even know until you went to pay your AMEX bill." She smiles something sinister, like the idea is enjoyable to her.

"There's a flaw in that plan."

"What?"

"You'll still be here. And I really couldn't give a shit if you take everything. As long as I have you and Graycee, I don't need anything else. She's not going to school."

"Okay, fine. You win. But we need to figure this out, because she is not becoming a homeschool kid." Kathryn throws her hands in the air with an exasperated huff.

"Why not? That's actually a really good idea. I could hire a full-time teacher... set up a little classroom."

"No, she needs to make friends. She needs to socialize with other kids."

"So let's give her a sibling then," I suggest with a grin.

Kathryn's eyes widen. "You have got to be kidding me. Please tell me you're joking." Her head shakes from side to side. "You're not joking, are you?" she presses when I don't say anything. "Oh my god. No! Grayson Monroe, I know it's not a word you hear very often, but *no*. We are not going to try to get pregnant while we have people coming after us."

"That's going to be sorted out real soon. I'm sure it won't take Dad and Vinny long to find the Duvals and put an end to their bullshit."

"Still, no. I got fat, Grayson. So fat. And the pain... it hurt."

"I think you'd be hot pregnant, and pregnant is not fat. As for the pain, I'll be there this time. We can do it together this time," I tell her. It might have been an off-the-cuff comment, but the more I'm thinking about it, the more I like the idea.

"How about we figure *us* out first? Let's get through this nightmare, come out the other end, and then enjoy just being us. You, me, and Graycee for a while."

"What if you're already pregnant? We haven't exactly done anything to prevent it," I remind her.

"Then we can deal with that when and *if* it happens, but do our best to not increase the odds anymore."

"Babe, you're already knocked up. I have strong sperm. One of those fuckers has gotten through an egg. Trust me."

Kathryn's face scrunches up before settling on a smirk. "That's just messed up, Gray, and you can be the one to tell Graycee she's not going to school."

"Easy." I lean over the kitchen counter and kiss Kathryn before I go in search of our daughter. I find her in the games room, sitting down at her little tea table. I walk over and lower myself opposite her. "What are you doing?"

"It's a tea party, Daddy. You want to play?" Graycee asks.

"I sure do."

She hands me a tiny pink cup. "You have to point your pinkie out. That's the rules," she tells me with the most serious expression on her face.

"Got it." I follow her instructions and sip at the empty cup. "Mmm, this is the best tea I've ever had." The big smile she offers in response melts my heart. So I use her good mood as my opening to breach the subject of staying home for a bit. "So I was thinking... You know how Daddy is on vacation from work? I thought it'd be cool to give you a little vacation from school too. You can hang out here with me and Mama for a while. How's that sound?"

"What would I do?" Graycee asks. "Can I still play hockey?"

"You can play as much hockey as you want. We own a whole arena, remember? But I think your hockey team is on break right now too."

"Oh, yeah. Can we go to The Castle today?"

"Today? I think that sounds like a stellar plan. Why don't you go get your skates and I'll tell Mama to get ready?" I push up on my knees before climbing to my feet. Then I hold out a hand for her to take.

"I think we should go to The Castle every day," Graycee says.

"Every day, huh? I'll see what I can do about that." It's really hard to say *no* to this girl.

We run into Kathryn on our way down the hallway. "Mama, we're going to The Castle to skate and play hockey!" Graycee announces before running off, her little curls bouncing behind her as she goes.

"So, that went well then?" Kathryn says. "Why are we going skating? You just finished the season yesterday."

"Because she asked, and I don't think I can say no to her," I admit. "How do you do it? You're going to have to teach me."

"You'll figure it out. Trust me." Kathryn rolls her eyes, and I grab her waist and tug her against me.

"You're going to want to put on some jeans and a sweater. We're going skating."

"I don't have skates," she says.

"We'll stop and get you some. I happen to know a great gear shop." I smirk.

"I haven't skated in six years, Grayson. I don't think I even remember how anymore."

"Yes, you can. It's like riding a bike. Besides, if you fall, I'll either catch you or laugh right before I pick your ass right back up. It could go either way, babe."

"Fine, but if I fall and get hurt, that's on you."

"You're not going to get hurt." I roll my eyes at her this time. I skated with Kathryn a lot back in the day. This woman could outmaneuver any of the guys on my team.

I drop my hands from her hips and watch her disappear down the hall towards our room to get changed, before taking out my phone and texting my father.

ME:

I'm heading over to The Castle with Kathryn and Graycee.

DAD:

Do not leave the house until Vinny gets there. He'll go with you.

ME:

I don't need a babysitter.

DAD:

It's a precaution, Grayson. Wait for your brother.

When Vinny shows up thirty or so minutes later, he's not alone. The fucker has a goddamn convoy in tow. Three SUVs.

"Get in," he says while holding the back door of the middle vehicle open.

"Over the top, bro. Even for you," I murmur as I help Graycee into her booster seat.

"We're not taking any chances, Grayson."

"I know. Thank you."

We stop to get Kathryn skates on the way over, much to my brother's annoyance, before pulling up to the arena like the royal family. Vinny is the first to enter through the door. Once he and his guys clear the building, the rest of us are ushered inside.

I help Graycee lace up her skates while Kathryn does her own. I don't miss the emotions that cross her face as she eyes the ice as though it might jump up and bite her. I don't think she's scared. But I can't quite put my finger on what it is she's feeling. However, something tells me that as soon as we're out there, everything is going to come back to her. And she's going to love it. Kathryn was always happiest with a pair of skates on her feet and the wind blowing through her hair. It was almost as if she felt freer somehow.

As soon as Graycee is properly laced up, she's off. The kid doesn't wait for anyone before her feet hit the ice. I sit next to Kathryn on the bench and get myself geared up. "Why do you look like you're about to dive into a pool of hungry sharks?"

"I'm just nervous."

"Why'd you stop skating? I mean, you had Graycee take lessons. Why didn't you teach her yourself?"

"I couldn't bring myself to get on the ice without you." Kathryn shrugs.

"Well, guess what?"

"What?"

"I'm right here, and the ice is right there. So we are getting on it. Together." I jump up and hold out a hand for her to take. Kathryn places her palm on mine, and I pull her upright. She doesn't wobble in the slightest. "Don't worry. I was only teasing. I promise I won't let you fall," I tell her.

"Thank you," she says.

I step onto the ice first, and Kathryn steps out after me while her hands are wrapped around mine in a death grip. "You do realize you can skate better than anyone else I know?"

She shakes her head. "It's just been a long time."

I pull her out to the middle of the rink and immediately drop my hands. Kathryn glares at me. She doesn't stumble though. I look down at her feet. They're steady.

Graycee skates over to us. "Mama, you can do it," she says, cheering Kathryn on.

"I can. Wanna help me do a lap, baby?"

"I can help you, Mama." Graycee grabs her mother's wrist, and I watch as they skate towards me. Kathryn looks back over her shoulder and holds out her hand for me to take. I don't think twice before accepting her invitation.

We do a whole lap around the rink at Graycee's pace, which is a lot slower than I'm used to, that's for sure. But also a nice change. My body is still recovering from yesterday's game.

"Wanna see something cool, Graycee baby?" Kathryn asks, then adds, "Something Daddy can't do."

"What?" Graycee peers up at us with renewed excitement.

Kathryn drops each of our hands and skates a little distance away. "Okay, obviously I haven't done this in a long time, so it's not going to be perfect," she says. "But watch."

Then she takes off down the ice, her movements so fucking graceful it's hard not to be awestruck. She turns around before lifting one leg into the air at a ninety-degree angle. When her foot hits the ice again, she goes into a spin, but not just any spin. One of those fancy twirls figure skaters do.

I knew Kathryn could skate. But I never knew she could dance like this. She's good. Even if she claims she's rusty. By the time she comes to a stop in front of Graycee and me again, Kathryn has a huge smile on her face and her chest rises and falls in rapid movements as she tries to catch her breath.

"That was so cool, Mama! Can you teach me how to do that?" Graycee squeals.

"Sure can, baby, but not all at once. It takes lots of time and practice," Kathryn tells her.

"That was amazing," I breathe out.

"Thank you."

I blink at her. That's it. *Thank you?* She's not going to tell me how she's an Olympic-level figure skater all of a sudden?

Kathryn sighs, as if reading my expression. "It's a long story," she says.

"Give me the Cliffs Notes' version," I tell her.

"My father wouldn't let me play hockey when I was younger. He put me in figure skating classes instead. Which I took right up until I went to college. After he passed away, I didn't have to pretend that I wanted to do it anymore."

"You sure didn't look like you hated it when you were out there, babe."

"I don't hate it as a whole. I just hated competing." She shrugs.

"Come on, dance with me," I say, then lean

down and tug Graycee into my arms. "You wanna dance with us, sweetheart?"

"Yes. Can we go fast?" she asks.

"Of course we can." I take Kathryn's hand and spin us around.

This is something I didn't know I was missing in my life. Having a daughter, having my girl back, letting go of that anger I've been holding in for all this time...

It makes me feel a whole lot lighter.

Chapter Thirty

I'm staring at a collection of faces. Men. Local law enforcement, to be more specific. Jacob and Vinny turned up with a folder full of images about half an hour ago, and I've been staring at picture after picture, trying to find the two detectives who took me in for questioning that day.

There are so many faces though, and they're starting to blur into the same image. I want to be able to do this for them so I keep on digging through.

"It's okay. Take your time, Kathryn," Gray says while resting a hand on my thigh.

I nod my head but continue looking. I have a huge pile of *not its*, and an empty space on the table where I intend to place the first picture I recognize. I flip through three more photos and then I see it. Him. One of them. It's a face I can't forget. He's what I'd call the bad cop, the one who was insistent on showing me what would happen if I didn't cooperate.

"Him," I say aloud and shoved the image across the table.

"You sure?" Jacob asks.

"I'm sure, Mr. Monroe. He was one of them."

I'm sifting through the pile in my hands, looking for the next guy, when Vinny stops me. "Kathryn, you can stop. It's okay," he says.

"But there were two men," I remind him.

"We can find the second guy by looking up this one's partner," Vinny explains.

"Oh. Okay." I set my pile on the table. I want to ask how they got all these pictures but I don't. I feel like this is a *the less I know, the better* kind of situation.

"I think you three should come and stay at the estate for a while," Jacob says after a long pause.

"Why?" Grayson asks.

"It's safer. Things are gonna start to get messier. So, until this is over, you should come down to the estate. Besides, Graycee hasn't been over yet and what kind of grandfather would I be if I didn't have my granddaughter in my home?"

I look to Grayson. I don't want to leave. We're settling into a good routine here. I don't like moving Graycee around unnecessarily. She's had to endure so much change over the last few months. I worry how it's all going to affect her.

"Okay, we'll come tonight." Gray sighs.

"Great. I've already had a room built for our girl," Jacob says.

As soon as Jacob and Vinny leave, I turn to Grayson. "What does he mean he had a room built?"

Gray shakes his head. "With my dad, who the fuck knows? It could be anything from simply redecorating a bedroom to building the kid a castle."

"Seriously?"

"*Seriously*. When I was twelve, I made a

comment about how I'd be a much better hockey player if I had an in-house rink to practice on."

"And?" I ask.

"A month later, I had one. My dad took out the swimming pool and turned that whole room into a rink."

"You have a rink in your family home? How did I miss that?"

"You didn't stay long enough for me to show you," Gray says, and my heart drops into my stomach with the reminder. "Knowing how much you and Graycee love skating, we should probably get one built here."

"That's insane. I can't believe you grew up with your own ice rink in your house. You really were a silver-spooner." I laugh.

"It wasn't always the glamourous life you'd imagine."

"I'm sure it wasn't." It's clear that being a Monroe comes with just as many challenges as it does perks. People always wanting a cut of the pie. I know better than anyone what it's like having to look over one shoulder and wonder who's out to get you.

"My mother tried to kill my sister when she was about Graycee's age. Well, actually, we came to learn she made a few attempts before that too," Gray says, and I can hear the pain in his voice.

"What?" This is the first time I've ever heard him talk about his mother.

"It's why I'm so fiercely protective of Aliyah. She had a really rough fucking start in life. Our mother did things to her that I can't even bear to think about, let alone say aloud. It was bad, Kathryn. But the worst part of it all was the fact that no one knew it was happening."

"How did you find out?"

"She sliced Aliyah's wrist with a knife in the bathroom, thinking Dad had taken us boys out for the day. But he forgot something at home and had to turn around. If he hadn't, I have no doubt Lia wouldn't be here with us..."

"Oh my god, I didn't know. I'm so sorry, Grayson..."

"It didn't happen to me," he says.

"It did. It happened to all of you. Yes, Aliyah got the brunt of it. But that kind of thing impacts everyone. Did your mother ever try to do something like that to you or your brothers?" I ask him.

"No, that's the weird part. I can't remember a time she even raised a hand to us. But Aliyah, she hated her. She was jealous of the attention my father gave her."

"That's horrible, Gray."

"Does it bother you?" He shifts his gaze from the floor, up to my face. Almost as if he's worried about what he may see staring back at him.

"What? That your mother was unstable? It's in the past, and you are not your mother."

"No, does it bother you how much attention I give Graycee?"

"What? Of course not! It would bother me if you didn't give her attention. If you brought us here and ignored her altogether, that would bother me." I shift onto my knees and climb into his lap. Taking his face in my hands, I tilt his head so his eyes meet mine again. "I love the relationship you're building with our daughter. It's more than I ever could have wished for. Because of you, she's going to know her worth as a woman. She's going to know how men should treat her in life. Because of you, she has a whole extended family who loves and adores her. I couldn't give her those things without you, Grayson."

"You know why she's such an awesome kid?" he says.

"Why?"

"Well, besides the fact she has Monroe blood

running through her veins, it's because you raised her right, Kathryn. You did an amazing job all on your own, under extremely difficult circumstances."

"Thank you." I lean my head against his shoulder and wrap my hands around the back of his neck. "Gray?"

"Yeah?"

"Why didn't you ever ask for a DNA test?"

His body stiffens underneath me. "Do I need to?"

"No, that's not what I meant. I mean, you just took my word that she was yours. Didn't you want proof?"

"I don't need proof, Kathryn. I know that girl is mine. She has my eyes. She's a Monroe through and through. There's no doubt about that. She's too awesome to belong to anyone else."

I smile. "Well, there are two Monroes I think are really awesome."

"Who?"

"You and Graycee. Who else?" I laugh at his glare.

"Just making sure. Though, now that you mention it, I should tell you something... Luke may have broken into your house, back when you were staying at your mom's, and he may have stolen a lock of Graycee's hair and sent it off for testing. I didn't know about any of it until after he came to me with the results." Gray sighs, like he's waiting for me to yell at him.

I should, but it's not anything I wouldn't expect from the overprotective men constantly hanging around this family. At the end of the day, it's good to know he has so many people in his corner.

"And let me guess? The results concluded that you are indeed the father?" I purse my lips.

"Yep."

"Shocking."

"I never doubted it, Kathryn. I mean that. The moment I saw that newspaper article, I knew. I could feel it."

"Why'd it take you so long to come for us then?" I ask him.

"I was waiting... I wasn't sure I would... I didn't know what to do. I guess I was also still in a little bit of shock. It was a lot to take in all at once."

"So, you what? Just forgot I was back. Until you didn't?"

"I might have stalked you a little," he says with an impish smirk.

"A little?" I raise a questioning brow.

"Okay, maybe a lot."

I lean my head back down on his shoulder and close my eyes. "Which reminds me... I have to do something with my mom's house."

"Yeah, I know. What do you want to do with it?"

"I don't know."

"We can wait. It doesn't need to be dealt with right now. *Right now*, what I need is you." His hands grip my hips and he pulls my core down onto his hard cock.

"Mama, Daddy, Poppy gave me an ice cream." Graycee comes running into the room, and Grayson groans, adjusting his pants when I climb off his lap.

"And you want another one?" I laugh at his discomfort while gesturing a thumb towards our daughter.

"I want another ten." He grins.

"Well, best be finding some other ovens to bake those in, because this one ain't it," I fire back while gesturing to my stomach.

"Never say never, babe."

"NEVER. I'm saying *never*, Grayson Monroe."

"Sorry. Can't hear you. Too busy listening to how someone was raiding my ice cream stash. I hope you left some for me, sweetheart." Gray stands and takes a few steps towards Graycee.

"I did. But then Uncle Vinny took it," she says.

"Vinny, I'm going to bring you down to the basement if you ate the last of my ice cream," Grayson yells as he walks out of the living room.

"What's in the basement, Mama?" Graycee asks me.

"Mmm, no idea. Ask Daddy," I tell her.

Huh, I guess this co-parenting thing really does have its benefits. It's nice not having to be the only one to answer all the questions. Now I can palm some of them off to Grayson.

Chapter Thirty-One

Grayson

I watch Kathryn and Liliana skate around with Graycee. I don't think my daughter has spent much time anywhere but on this ice, since we came to my father's house a few days ago.

Liliana tagged along because she refuses to leave Kathryn's side. And because Liliana *tagged along*, so did her father, brother, and cousin. To say the estate is bursting at the seams is an understatement. The Valentinos have their own space in town. But for some reason, every time I turn around, I run into one of them here.

Speaking of...

"She's good," Theo says, stepping up next to me, his eyes glued to my daughter as she practices the figure skating move Kathryn taught her the other day.

"Yeah, she is." I grin.

"She reminds me of you, when you were that age. It was hard for your parents to get you off the ice too."

"Lucky for her, both Kathryn and I love being out on the ice just as much." I turn to look at him. "Any news on the Duvals?"

Theo and my father have joined forces to find these assholes. They've gone underground. Probably know their time is coming to an end. No one has seen or heard from them—well, at least no one who's prepared to talk. Vinny has been hitting the streets hard, searching for anyone with known ties to that family. It's funny how quickly everyone's memory fades when they're asked questions they don't want to answer.

"Nothing yet, but come on. Your pops wants to see you." Theo taps my shoulder as he walks out.

I follow behind him, taking two steps into my father's office only to find it full. Vinny is leaning up against the bookshelves on the far end of the room. Alessandro and Enzo stand next to each other by the door, and Theo sits across from my dad on one of the matching black leather sofas.

"You summoned me?" I ask.

"Yeah, we found the detective," he says while patting the spot next to him.

I take a seat. "Great, where the fuck is he?"

"Not so fast. Check out the name." He hands me a sheet of paper, the photo that Kathryn picked out the other day, and under the man's makeshift mugshot is a name. Detective Logan Hughes.

"Hughes? Any connection to Brendan Hughes?" I ask.

Brendan Hughes is the current captain of the Nashville Jets. He's also the same fucker who took the position I had my eye on back in college when I went off the rails after Kathryn's disappearance. He was a fucking asshole back then and still is now.

"His brother," Dad says.

"Brother? Brendan never mentioned having a

brother. I played on the same team with him for four years."

"Different mothers, same father. But they're brothers all right."

"Logan is on the Duval's payroll, has been for as long as I can remember. Although, from what I can tell, it's more like the Duvals work for him. I don't know what the fucker has on them but he's been using them to do his dirty work for decades," Theo says.

"You think Brendan had something to do with the Duvals trying to blackmail us into throwing the game?" It'd make sense if that's the case. Brendon knew the only way he'd win against me was if they cheated.

"I don't know. The Duvals lost five mil on that game. It could have just been a money grab. If the Cup went to Nashville, they would have pocketed twenty," Dad says.

"Well, there's only one way to find out? Right? Why are we all sitting around here with our thumbs up our asses? We need to fucking hunt 'em down and ask them." I jump up, ready to get this shitshow on the road.

"Don't move," Vinny snaps. "We need a plan,

Gray." His phone rings before he can say more, and he walks out of the room to answer it.

"A plan? Dad, these assholes came after my daughter. After the mother of my child. The longer they're out there, the more of a threat they become." My voice rises to near shouting.

"You wanna play at being a made man? Go for it. You'll end up with a bullet between your eyes in five minutes. You're a hockey player, Grayson. Let the experts handle this," Alessandro grunts.

I turn to him. My eyes travel up and down the length of his body, sizing him up. He's not a small kid by any means, but like he said, I'm a hockey player. I can fucking take him and win. "Wanna put your money where your mouth is, wise guy? Five hundred says I'll have you on the ground within a minute."

"Wise guy? Seriously?" Alessandro chuckles. "Okay, let's do this." He unbuttons the jacket of his custom-made suit and shrugs out of it.

My brother walks back into the room as the cocky bastard steps toe-to-toe with me. "We gotta head over to Gray's. His place was broken in to while we were gone," Vinny says.

"How the fuck did that happen? There are guards all over that house."

"There *were* guards all over that house," Vinny mutters under his breath. "Now, come on."

I walk through the busted-in front door. My dad and Vinny are next to me, with Alessandro following behind us. Theo and Enzo stayed back at my father's estate. I didn't want to leave Kathryn and Graycee there without me. But, fuck, I'm glad I didn't bring them here to see this.

The place is trashed. Glass crunches with every step I take into the foyer. I look to my right, into the living room, where sofas are turned up and cushions are ripped open. The flat screen that was on the wall is now on the ground in pieces.

"Don't think they found what they were looking for," Alessandro comments.

"What the fuck were they looking for?" I ask aloud.

"My guess? Nothing. They just want you to know they can get in," Vinny tells me.

I turn and head upstairs, my dad's heavy footsteps stomping behind me. There is nothing in this house that can't be replaced. I'm just fucking glad that Graycee and Kathryn were not here.

I walk into my daughter's bedroom first, and my blood boils over at the sight. What kind of fucking animals destroy a little girl's room?

"Fuck."

I hear my dad curse under his breath and shift my focus to what he's looking at. They've spray painted a message on the wall.

> *Graycee,*
> *You hide. I'll seek.*
> *1, 2, 3… I'm coming to find you.*

"Dad?" I don't know what to say. This is a direct threat against my daughter.

"I know," he grunts as one of his hands lands on my shoulder. "We aren't going to let anything happen to her. We will find them."

I swallow the lump in my throat. "What do I do?"

"You go home and you act like everything is fine. The last thing you want is to spook Kathryn and have her run off again," Dad says.

I shake my head. "I'm going to help you find these assholes, and when we do, I'm going to make sure the whole fucking city knows not to threaten my fucking daughter." Then I barge past Alessandro on my way out of the room. I need to get home. I call Kathryn before I make it to the bottom of the stairs.

"Hey."

"Hey, is Graycee with you?" I ask her.

"Yes, where else would she be, Gray?"

"Can I talk to her?" I need to talk to her more than anything else right now.

"Sure, hang on."

"Hello, Daddy." Graycee's sweet voice comes through the speaker, and I can finally breathe again.

"Graycee, sweetheart, how you doing?" I ask her.

"Good. We're getting ready to skate with Aunt Lil."

"Oh, fun. Don't wear yourself out. I want to skate with my favorite girl when I get home," I tell her.

"Okay, I won't."

"Give Mama the phone back. I love you."

"Love you too, Daddy."

"Gray? Is everything okay?" Kathryn asks a moment later.

"Yeah, it's good. I'm just going to stop by the hospital and see Aliyah. I'll be home soon."

"Okay, I'll see you soon." Kathryn cuts the call by the time I get to my car.

When I turn around, Alessandro is already standing behind me. "I'll come with you. It's been ages since I've seen your sister," he says.

I shrug. "Suit yourself. But be warned... her boyfriend's a dick."

"I'm finding most hockey players are." The fucker smirks at me, and I flip him the bird.

"Get in or find your own damn way there."

The first thing I notice at the hospital is all the men my dad has standing around the place. I knock on the door before walking into King's room. Aliyah is asleep on his bed. King looks at me and smiles.

"I knew you'd miss me," he whispers.

"Fuck off. I came to see my sister, not your ugly ass," I tell him.

Aliyah's eyes blink open. "Gray? What are you doing here?" She sits up and looks at King. "Are you okay?"

"I'm good. You?" he asks her.

"Mmhmm." Aliyah pushes off the bed and walks over to me. Her arms wrap around my waist and she tugs me close. "How are you?"

I hold her tight. "I'm good. What about you, Lia?" I ask and press my lips to the top of her head.

"I'd be better if my boyfriend wasn't laid up in a hospital bed with a bullet hole in his body," she says.

"I'd be better if he wasn't your boyfriend," I counter.

Aliyah steps back, only to whack me in the stomach in the process. Her eyes then go to the person standing behind me. "Alessandro! Oh my god! What are you doing here? When did you get here?" she squeals, shoving me out of the way to get to him. She throws her arms around his neck, and

Alessandro picks her up, spinning her around before setting her feet back on the ground.

I smirk when I hear the growl coming from King, who is about ready to jump out of his hospital bed. "They're old friends," I tell him, then add, "*Super-close,* old friends." The fucker does not smile, his eyes still focused on Alessandro like he wants to kill the guy. I lean down and whisper, "I'd advise against whatever it is you're thinking. Not only would he likely knock your ass out first, but his last name's Valentino."

"What is it with that family putting their hands all over your sister?" King grunts, and I ignore him. It's about time the bastard felt a little bit of my pain.

"I got here a few days ago. Lil came to town. Pops and I followed her, and Enzo followed us," Alessandro says. He holds Aliyah back and looks her up and down. "You look good, Lia. Real good." He smirks.

Aliyah blushes. Actually fucking blushes. If I didn't know better, I'd strangle Alessandro myself right now, but I know he's not interested in my sister like that. She did, however, have the biggest crush on him back when they were thirteen.

"Enzo's here too? Where is he?" Aliyah asks.

"At your dad's place," Alessandro says and then

finally shifts his gaze over to King. He smiles, fucking huge, and wraps an arm around my sister's shoulders. "What's this I hear about you having yourself a boyfriend? I thought you were saving yourself for me, *bella*?"

"I'm going to fucking rip your arm off your body," King snarls.

Alessandro bends over in pain after catching an elbow to the ribs from Aliyah. "Ignore him, Liam. He's an idiot. And trying to get under your skin." She moves back to King's bedside and gestures a hand between the two men. "Alessandro, this is Liam. My future fiancé."

"Future fiancé? Why future?" Alessandro asks.

"Because he hasn't asked me properly yet." Aliyah smiles.

"I'm actually a huge fan," Alessandro tells Liam, likely looking to appease my sister and lighten the mood. "I was hoping you'd get picked up by New York, but I guess the Knights aren't too bad either."

"Not too bad? We just fucking won the Stanley Cup, ass," I hiss.

"Thanks," King says to Alessandro, still eyeing the fucker like he's ready to kill him.

"Lia, I'll come back tomorrow. You need anything from home?" I ask her.

"Yeah, some clothes, but can you ask Kathryn to pack them? I don't want you going through my wardrobe," she says.

"Sure." I lean down and kiss her cheek, then grab Alessandro's arm and pull him out of the room. "Come on, let's go before he actually does try to kill you and I have to help him," I say.

"You'd help him?" Alessandro's head snaps in my direction.

"It's the code. Also, if I let you kill him, it'd leave my sister heartbroken."

"Don't worry. She wouldn't be heartbroken for long." Alessandro laughs.

"You're an ass," I tell him.

"Never pretended to be anything else," he says with a grin.

Chapter Thirty-Two

Kathryn

"Mmm," I moan as my hips gyrate, "Gray, oh shit. Don't stop." My hands move up my body and cup my breasts. Pinching my own nipples between my fingers. He's always had a magical tongue, even in my dreams.

"Fuck, you taste so fucking good," he says. The blanket lifts off me and my eyes pop open.

"This isn't a dream," I realize as my gaze meets his. Gray's head is currently buried between my thighs.

"Speak for yourself. Your cunt is my very definition of a dream, babe," he says.

"Don't stop," I repeat as my spine arches off the bed. Gray's tongue slides back up through the lips of my pussy, and he circles it around my clit, then flattens it out, lapping at me like he's licking his favorite dessert.

My head tips back and my eyes close. Gray's fingers dig into the flesh of my thighs, pinning me down to the mattress. And I swear this is the way I want to wake up for the rest of my life. My fingers pull and tug harder on my nipples through the satiny fabric of my nightgown.

"Oh shit," I cry out and then cover my mouth with a hand. I don't need the whole house to know what Gray's doing to me in here.

He shifts his weight and then I feel his hand move up my thigh. His fingers glide through my folds before he shoves two into my opening. Gray latches on to my clit with his mouth, alternating between sucking, licking, and nibbling while those two fingers pump in and out of me.

My hips push up, grinding against his hand and face harder, chasing that release that's so close. My thighs shake, my whole body alight with pleasure. And then, like a bomb, I detonate and fly off into a state of pure orgasmic bliss.

Gray climbs over me. "I missed this," he says as his lips press to mine.

I wrap my arms around his neck. "Me too." I can't help the ridiculously happy smile that graces my face. Then I feel his cock at my entrance as he slowly thrusts forward. "Gray, condom."

He stops and looks at me. "Seriously?"

"*Seriously*. I'm not on birth control," I remind him for the millionth time.

"It's already too late for that, but if it makes you feel better, I'll pull out." He grins in a way that tells me I shouldn't believe him.

I know it's stupid, but I nod my head. It's the very opposite of what I should be doing right now, but I've never been good at saying no to Gray in the bedroom. It's not just pregnancy that I'm at risk of, though. It's diseases. My damn health is on the line.

"I swear to God, Grayson Monroe, if you've

given me an STD, I'm going to cut your dick off," I tell him.

"Babe, I'm as clean as a whistle. I've never fucked anyone bare but you. I'm not a total moron," he says.

"You're trying to knock me up after we've only just gotten back together. That's pretty moronic, if you ask me."

"Good thing no one's asking you then," he says, pulling out and sinking back in.

"Wait." My hands press against his chest.

Gray groans. "What now?"

"Are we?" I ask.

"Are we what?"

"Back together? What are we doing here, Gray?"

He blinks at me. "We are very much back together. You are mine, Kathryn. Mine," he says.

"Okay, but are you mine?"

"I've always been yours." He lowers his lips. "I love you," he whispers into my mouth.

"Mmm, I love you too," I tell him.

Gray starts moving in and out of me again. Slowly. And I push against his chest. Again. This time, rolling us over. Once I'm on top, I sit up and my hands roam along his torso. Flattening my palms out on his pecs. My fingers curl, digging into his skin as I use my knees to lift myself up and drop onto him.

I feel the tip of his cock hit that sweet spot deep inside me. Repeating the motion, I lift myself up and fall back down, grinding my clit against his pelvic bone as he bottoms out. Gray's hands cup my breasts, massaging the flesh between his fingers. One of his hands moves up my chest to my throat. He doesn't add any pressure, though, just rests it there. His large palm wrapped around my neck like a choker chain. I lean into his hold. I want him to squeeze.

"Choke me," I tell him.

He looks at me with something akin to fear in his eyes. "Last time I did that, I almost killed you, Kathryn," he says.

I continue moving up and down on his cock. "You wouldn't have. I trust you, Grayson. Please," I plead with him.

His hand tightens a little and I feel it instantly. I don't know how to explain it, but it's something that only happens when he has that hand wrapped around my neck. My pussy floods with arousal, and my whole being ignites. And it doesn't take long before I'm coming again. My body collapses on top of Gray's as he runs a hand up and down my back in soothing motions. When I've caught my breath, he rolls us back over.

Rising to his knees, he lifts both of my legs in the

air, holds my ankles against his right shoulder, and thrusts into me. His movements hard, relentless, as he fucks me. Just when I think I'm going to die a torturous but pleasurable death, he groans and pulls out. Then he drops my legs, grabs his cock, and pumps it before his cum squirts out all over my stomach. When he's finished, Gray swipes a finger through the mess and writes something across my skin.

"What are you writing?" I ask him.

"Mine," he says with a quirk of his lips while flashing that damn dimple at me.

"He's so good with her," Liliana says.

We're watching Gray and Graycee play together in the room that Jacob built for his granddaughter. If I thought Gray went overboard on buying her shit, then his dad has gone that times ten. This isn't just a room. It's an indoor play area. Kind of like the ones you see at McDonald's. Only this one is probably three times the size. And it's pink and purple everywhere. Graycee loves it, though. She says she wants to live here forever. Between the ice rink and this playroom, she has everything a kid her age could ever want.

"He is. I always knew he would be," I tell Liliana.

"You know, it's okay to let yourself be happy too, Kathryn."

"I am happy." I smile.

"No, you're not. I know you, and you're still holding back."

"I'm worried—that's all. And I'm not holding back. I'm just... being cautiously distant," I try to explain.

"Worried about what?" she asks.

"Graycee, Gray, take your pick. I'm worried that I've put everyone I love in danger, and there isn't anything I can do to fix it or keep them safe," I admit.

"Sometimes we have to let other people fix things. Not everything is for us to do alone."

"Speaking like a true feminist there, Lil." I laugh. "What happened to the girl in college who was adamant that she was never going to ask a man for anything?"

"She grew up and learned that it's okay to ask for help when you need it." Liliana shrugs.

"It's not that I don't want to let people help. It's just the realization that if it weren't for me, none of this would be happening."

"You're right, but if it weren't for you, we also wouldn't have that amazing little girl." Liliana nods towards Graycee. "I wouldn't have my best friend, and Gray wouldn't have his soul mate."

"I don't know how you can just forgive me so easily. How we cannot see each other for years, but when I'm with you, it's like no time has passed at all."

"That's because you and I are the real soul mates. I'm just going to let Grayson keep thinking otherwise. Because he's a grouch and likely about to be my boyfriend's team captain."

"Back up. What the actual F-U-C-K, Lil? You're moving to Vancouver?" I squeal.

"Well, Travis is. I think. Me? I have to try to get my mom to do her magic voodoo shit on my dad, so he doesn't burn the whole of Vancouver down when he finds out."

"Oh my god! I'm so excited. This is the best news

I've had in, well, a long time." I wrap my arms around her.

"What's the best news?" Gray asks, his head shooting up to look in our direction.

"Liliana is moving to Vancouver!" I squeal again. "Isn't that great?"

"Travis is gonna accept the trade?" His eyes bounce to Liliana now.

"I don't know what you're talking about." She smiles.

"Right. Gotcha." Gray chuckles and goes back to Graycee, who's already calling him out for being distracted during playtime.

Chapter Thirty-Three

Bang! Bang! Bang!

Some fucker is pounding on the bedroom door. Kathryn groans from where she's lying next to me. She pulls the covers over her head. "Make 'em go away."

I get up, less than half-awake, and find that the

door isn't even shut properly. We usually leave it ajar so Graycee can get in easily in the mornings.

"What the fuck are you doing? Trying to wake Jesus?" I ask Vinny.

"Nope, just your sorry ass. Get dressed and meet me downstairs. Don't wear anything you don't want to burn afterwards," he says.

"What the fuck? What's going on?"

"Just meet me downstairs." He turns and walks down the hallway.

After going to the bathroom, I throw on a pair of sweats and a Knights shirt. Then I slide my feet into a pair of runners and head downstairs.

It doesn't take me long to find my brother. Except he's not alone. He has Brendan Hughes next to him. I look from Vinny to my former teammate. "What's going on?"

"You tell me. Your brother claimed it was a matter of life and death and that I had no choice but to come here with him. To see you," Brendan grunts.

"It is a matter of life and death," Vinny confirms, before pulling a nine from behind his back and making a scene of checking the chamber. He then points the barrel directly at Hughes's head.

"What the fuck?" Brendan takes a step back, his hands thrown in the air like it'll do him any good.

"Can we take this somewhere else?" I ask Vinny. My fucking daughter is in the house, and this is the last thing I want her seeing.

"Turn around. Walk," Vinny says to Brendan, then calls over one shoulder to me, "Gray, show him where the basement is."

I glare at my brother. He knows damn well that's not what I meant. But I guess the basement is better than the middle of the goddamn living room. Then I shake my head and lead the way as Vinny shoves Brendan forward in front of him and behind me.

As soon as we make it down the stairs, I realize this was the plan all along. My dad, Theo, Alessandro, and Enzo are all here waiting.

Vinny pushes Brendan towards the chair. "Sit."

Brendan's face pales. Goes ghostly white. And he looks like he's about to fucking piss himself. Once he's sitting, Alessandro steps up, takes hold of my former teammate's wrists, and ties them behind the chair while Enzo wraps rope around each of the guy's ankles, securing his legs in place.

"Done that a few times?" I quirk a brow in question.

"Once or twice." Enzo chuckles.

"You know why you're here?" Vinny asks Brendan.

"Fuck off. I didn't do shit. Let me go!" he screams.

"Okay, I will. Right after you tell me where your brother is."

Brendan's eyes widen and he swallows. "I don't have a brother." Then he looks to me. "Come on, Gray, what the fuck is this?"

"You sure you don't have a brother? Because I could have sworn you did. Goes by the name Detective Logan Hughes. Ring a bell?" I ask him.

"I'm not telling you shit," Brendan hisses before tugging his arms and legs to no avail. The fucker ain't going nowhere anytime soon.

"Want your stick?" Vinny grins as he offers up my hockey gear.

Then Alessandro drops a bag of pucks onto the ground. "I've been dying to see this ever since I heard about it," he says. "Two of my favorite blood sports rolled up in one. Can't think of a better time."

I dribble a puck in front of me and take a small step back. "I don't have to tell you how much this is gonna hurt. You already know," I tell Brendan. "But I will give you one last shot at avoiding all the drama. Where's your brother?"

"I don't know," he repeats. I snap my stick back and swing. The puck lands across his chest. "Fuck!"

He clenches his jaw as he breathes in and out through his mouth. He's a hockey player. We're used to dealing with pain. Which means it's going to take more than one slapshot to break him.

I take my time lining up ten of the black disks while Brendan eyes each one. "You sure you don't know where that brother is?" I ask him again.

"Fuck you, Monroe."

"Don't say I didn't warn you," I say before going hard and fast, firing puck after puck at him in rapid succession.

"Okay, okay! Fuck, stop! I'll tell you!"

I look down. I have three left. Guess he's not as tough as I thought.

"He's in a shitty motel, that one on the way into town, on the east side."

"I'm gonna need more than that, Hughes," I tell him, dribbling the next puck in my line.

"I don't know the name of the place. It's got that big V over the building," he says quickly.

"One more question. Why is your brother after Kathryn?"

"He's not. He wouldn't hurt her." Brendan shakes his head back and forth.

"Why not? He interviewed her, six years ago, scared her to death and sent her into hiding. Why?"

"It was nothing," Brendan says. "I swear. We were just kids, Gray, young and stupid."

I take a step closer to him. "What did you do?"

Brendan shakes his head again.

"Give me a gun." I hold out a hand. When nothing lands on my palm, I turn and glare at my father and brother. "Seriously? Someone give me a fucking gun."

"We got what we needed, Gray," Vinny says.

"No, we didn't," I growl out between clenched teeth, and Alessandro shoves a nine in my direction.

"Here."

"Thank you." I take it with a little more force than necessary and switch off the safety. Then I press the hot end under Brendan's chin. "Why, Hughes? What the fuck did you do six years ago?" I ask again.

"I didn't mean it. I just... I saw Kathryn in the library. I saw what she was doing on her computer and I told my brother. I told him she was the key to getting you out of the way so I could get the captain spot. I didn't know anything else he did. I wouldn't hurt her," he says.

"You told your brother to threaten her so you could have a fucking captain slot on a goddamn college hockey team?"

"She wasn't supposed to leave. You were. She was supposed to stay. I would have helped her. I can still help her. I love her. I can help her," he says over and over again.

My eyes widen as blood splatters all over my face. I look at what's left of Brendan's skull, not able to recall pulling the trigger. Then I step back and hand the gun to Alessandro. My dad passes me a towel so I can wipe away the gore dripping from my nose and eyebrows.

"Let's go get this detective," I tell him.

Half an hour later, we're parked out front of some seedy motel. "Why is he hiding out here if the Duvals are in his pocket?" I grunt.

"No fucking idea," Dad says before stepping out of the car. "Let us handle it this time, Grayson."

347

"I'm actually a little impressed. I thought the only things you were good at were hockey, fighting, and drinking," Alessandro tells me with a cocky-ass smirk on his face.

I glare at him. I'm not looking for his fucking approval. Nor do I need it. I shake my head and follow my dad and the Valentinos up to the door, expecting one of them to knock. Theo lifts his foot and kicks the door down instead.

"That's one way to do it, I guess," I murmur.

"Why knock when you can make a statement?" Enzo grins.

We find Logan Hughes on the bed, a bottle of Jack hanging loosely in one hand and a remote in the other. "I thought you'd be here sooner," he slurs.

"Had a stop to make first," Theo tells him. "You know who I am?"

Logan's eyes widen and he nods. "I know who you are."

"Good, so then you also know I'm not going to waste my time. I don't play with my food. Tell me where the sons of bitches are hiding out, and we'll leave quieter than we came in."

"I can't tell you that. They'll kill me," Logan stutters.

"And we won't?" Dad asks him.

"You will, but at least I won't die a traitor if you do it." Logan closes his eyes for a minute, the alcohol likely dulling his senses, before they snap back open again. "You know, I came to you. Twenty years ago. I offered you my services and you laughed in my face. Guess you're regretting that decision now, huh?"

"There are very few things I regret in life. *That* is not one of them. Where are the Duvals?"

"I don't know." Logan shrugs.

"Wrong answer," Theo says, pulling the trigger on a gun I didn't even see him take out from wherever he was concealing it. The bullet hits the fucker's kneecap.

Logan screams and my first thought is: *Fuck, even his little brother was tougher*.

"I don't know. You might as well kill me. I'm not going to tell you," he says. "But they'll find her, you know. You can't protect her."

"Who?" I ask.

"Your daughter and her bitch of a mother. This is all her fault. If she just cooperated back then, none of this would be happening now."

I turn to Theo. "Either you shoot him or give me the gun and I'll do it my-fucking-self."

I hear the gunshot and then look back at Logan,

who is now flat on the bed with a gaping hole between his eyes.

"Call a cleaner in. Find anything this asshole has on him. Search his phone, laptop, everything. He'll have something on where those fuckers are hiding out," Theo tells his son and nephew.

"Sure thing, Pops." Alessandro nods his head and pivots on his heel with a phone already pressed to one ear.

Chapter Thirty-Four

I spot Gray the moment he walks into the house. He goes straight upstairs.

"Lil, can you watch Graycee for a sec?" I say.

"Like you even have to ask." Liliana rolls her eyes at me.

"You're the best," I throw over one shoulder before running out of the room and up the stairs after him.

I woke up and Gray was gone. No note or anything to tell me where he went. Graycee has been asking for him all morning, and I've had no idea what to tell her other than he'll be back soon.

I walk into the bedroom and open the bathroom door. Gray's eyes meet mine through the reflection of the mirror. He's covered in blood. So much blood.

"What happened? Are you hurt? Where?" I turn him around and start tugging at his shirt. "Grayson, where are you hurt?" I yell at him when he doesn't answer me the first time.

He takes hold of my hands. "I'm fine. It's not my blood," he says, squeezing tight.

"What do you mean it's not your blood? Grayson, it's all over you." I try to tug my arms free. I need to get his shirt off. I need to see where he's hurt.

"I killed someone." Gray whispers the words, almost like he doesn't want me to hear them but has to say them anyway.

I freeze. My eyes meet his. "What do you mean you killed someone? How?"

"You don't want to know how, Kathryn. I just... I couldn't stop myself," he says.

"It's okay. We can figure this out. What do you need? What do we do? Gray, I can't lose you again. I just got you back. Graycee can't lose you," I tell him. I know it's selfish to be thinking about myself when clearly he's so messed up, but shit...

What the hell am I supposed to say?

"Babe, I'm not going anywhere. You're not going to lose me."

"You don't know that. What if the police..." I shake my head. "What happened?" I finally snap my hands free, reach in the shower, and turn on the water.

"Remember Brendan Hughes from college?" Gray asks.

"You mean the Nashville captain? That Brendan Hughes?"

"Yep, that one. The detective who took you in... was his brother. I don't know. Brendan saw you in the library or some shit like that. He wanted to get rid of me. That was his goal. He wanted the captain position and he wanted you," Gray says.

"So his brother made all of it up? The Duvals. All those murders?"

"Kathryn, I didn't kill those people. Up until a few days ago, I'd never killed anyone."

"A few days ago?"

"Someone tried to break into the house. Vinny had 'em in the basement. I don't know what came over me, Kathryn, but the thought of someone coming after you and Graycee... It just... turns me into someone I never thought I'd be," he says.

"Okay. You're okay. Graycee is okay. We're going to be okay," I repeat. "Take off your clothes."

"Kathryn, I killed someone. Two someones." Gray's brows knit together as he looks me in the eye and tries to read my reaction.

"I know. So you've told me."

"Why aren't you freaking out?"

"Because if it's a *you or them* situation, Grayson, I want you... *need* you to always pick you. We need you. You didn't kill anyone. You protected your family. There is a difference. Now, come on. Get in the shower. Graycee has been waiting for you to come home all morning," I tell him.

"I don't want you to be scared of me. I don't want you to think I'm someone I'm not." He pulls his shirt over his head. There's so much blood on him I'm starting to get dizzy.

"I'm not scared of you, Gray." I force down the acid and try to regain my bearings. "And I know exactly who you are. Get in the shower."

"Who am I?"

"You are Grayson Monroe, a Stanley Cup champion. A father, a damn good one too. You're my..." I pause, wondering what title is appropriate. "You're my person, Gray. You're my soul mate. But don't tell Lil that because she really does think that's her spot. And you are a good man. You're caring, loyal, and fiercely protective of the people you love. Can you be an ass at times? Sure." I smile and Grayson frowns at me. "But you're an ass I happen to love and really don't want to have to go back to living without. Ever again," I tell him.

"You won't have to. You're right. You and I are soul mates. I'm getting that fucking tattooed on me. And Lil can get in line, because I'm not giving that title up to anyone."

"Okay. You shower. I'm going to go burn these clothes."

"How'd you know you have to burn them?" he asks me.

"I've seen movies, Grayson. I'm not a complete idiot." I scoop up the bloody clothes and walk out the door.

I use the back stairs, to avoid running into Graycee, and head into the library. I know there's a fireplace in there. Dropping the clothes on the floor, I look around and find the fire starters and lighter.

Once the flames are going, and small bits of kindling are burning bright, I shove the clothes inside and watch them burn.

My mind is whirling with what Gray just told me as I sit cross-legged in front of the mantle. He killed people. Because of me. I've turned him into a killer.

"You okay?"

I jump at the sound of the voice, and my hand lands on my chest as I spin my head around. Gray's dad is there. Just standing in the room, staring down at me. "Ah, yeah, sorry. I just wanted to warm up a bit," I tell him.

"What are you burning in there?" He dips his head towards the fireplace.

Shit. Does he know? Did Gray tell him? I should have asked more questions.

"Ah, just an old dress. It was my mom's and seeing it makes me sad," I lie.

Jacob smiles. "You really do love him, don't you?"

"Grayson? Yes, I do."

"Good. He's going to need it. That sort of love and loyalty. He's going to need you to anchor him. It's never easy the first time," Jacob says and walks out.

Guess that gives me my answer. He does know. I

return my focus to the fireplace. I'm not leaving this room until there is nothing but ashes left.

I don't know how long I've been sitting here before Gray comes and positions himself behind me, a large leg on each side of mine, and then wraps his arms around my chest. My back rests against him. I lean my head on his shoulder.

"I'm sorry," he says.

"For what?"

"For putting this burden on you. I didn't want you to know."

"I'm glad you did, Grayson. We don't need to have secrets between us," I tell him. "I mean, look what my secret did to us... I wish I just told you what happened back then."

"It happened, and we're past it," he says.

"Promise me something." I turn in his arms to face him.

"Anything."

"Promise me that you'll talk to me. If you need to. Like if you struggle. Or, I don't know, feel remorse or something. Which would be totally normal, by the way. Just... don't keep it in. Talk to me."

"I promise I will talk to you. But the thing is... I don't feel anything but relieved that two of our problems are gone. Once my father and Theo find the

Duvals, it'll all be over and we can go home. And then we can finally take Graycee on that Disney trip."

"That sounds like a dream." I turn around again and lean my back on his chest.

"It sure does," Gray says, kissing the top of my head.

Chapter Thirty-Five

Grayson

I sit down with Graycee at the breakfast table. One of the benefits of being at my father's place is the fact that he has full-time cooks on staff. I might actually have to steal one of them. The woman makes the best pancakes, and watching Graycee's face light up every time she sees them on the table is like witnessing a rainbow after days of pouring rain.

"Daddy, do you want pancakes too?" Graycee asks.

"Absolutely, I do. I love these pancakes," I say while filling her plate, then my own.

"They're sooo good." She smiles up at me.

"You know, we might have to steal Poppy's chef. Take her home with us when we leave here," I joke.

"Mama says stealing is bad."

"It is bad, baby. I was kidding." *Mostly.*

"Daddy, when are we going home?"

"Soon. I thought you were having fun here?"

"I like Poppy's house. Your house doesn't have ice," she says.

"It's *our* house, not my house, baby. And I'll build you your very own rink too. I'll make sure it's even bigger than Poppy's," I tell her.

"Really? Like at The Castle?"

"Maybe not that big, but we'll see what we can do."

"That's a bit extreme, Grayson. She doesn't need her own skating rink," Kathryn tells me from across the table.

"She doesn't have to need it to want it, babe." I grin.

"You're going to spoil her, and it's gonna come back to bite you in the ass when she's a teenager," Kathryn says.

"Impossible, because I'll just keep spoiling her." I smile and Kathryn rolls her eyes, while Graycee ignores us both as she digs into her pancakes.

"When do you think we can go back to your place?" Kathryn asks.

"Soon. We need to do some redecorating. I've got cleaners there at the moment, clearing the place out," I tell her.

"Why?"

"It was ransacked." I fill my mouth with a forkful of the fluffiest pancakes and groan without meaning to.

Kathryn's eyes widen. "What? When? Again? What?"

"I'm dealing with it." I wave a dismissive hand and return my focus to the plate in front of me. Until my phone buzzes on the table with a message from my dad and I toss my fork down with an audible clatter.

DAD:

Come to The Castle. Alone.

ME:

Why?

DAD:

Just get here, Grayson.

"I have to go meet my dad. You remember where the rooms are, right?" I've asked her this a million times. If she remembers where the hidden panic rooms are in my father's estate. I've made her demonstrate how to get into them as well.

"I remember."

She thinks they're not needed. That it's over the top. I haven't had the heart to tell her about the time this house was breached. Only a few weeks before I found Kathryn, Aliyah and Liam were forced to hide in one of those rooms. It's probably what saved both of their lives.

"We'll be fine, Gray," Kathryn says.

"I know." I push my chair out from the table, lean down, and kiss my daughter on the head. "I'll be back as soon as I can."

"Okay, Daddy," Graycee says with bits of pancake falling out of her mouth.

Then I walk around the table, take hold of Kathryn's chin, and press my lips to hers. "I love you."

"I love you," she replies, then adds, "Don't do anything that could take you away from us."

"Never." I wink at her.

I've walked into this arena more times than I can count. This place has been my second home for as long as I can remember. But never in my life have I walked in on a scene like what I'm looking at right now.

There are five chairs set up in the middle of the ice. Each holding a different member of the Duval family. Four sons and a father, David Duval. All of 'em look like they've seen better days.

I step up next to my dad, eyeing each of the fuckers responsible for attacking my family. For threatening my fucking daughter. For ensuring I missed six years of her life. For helping take her mother away from me all those years ago.

"We've been waiting for you," Dad says.

"For what?" I ask him.

"For the fun to begin." Theo smiles, and I have to do a double take. It's fucking scary shit when a man who never smiles finally does. Almost like his facial muscles aren't used to it and contort at a weird angle.

"Now that we're all here, let's get this show on the road." My father takes a measured step towards the Duvals. The man can even make walking look threatening.

"Fuck you." David Duval spits at dad's polished shoes.

"Fuck me? You see, the mistake you made was coming after my kids. My daughter, my granddaughter. So, no, *fuck you*." My father's right hook connects with the side of Duval's face, snapping the man's head backwards on impact.

Blood splatters onto the ice. The contrast of red against white might be grotesque to some but it's not foreign to me. I want to see this whole rink stained with these fuckers' blood.

"I was doing what I had to do. It wasn't personal," Duval says.

This gives me pause. "Why?"

"Fucking Hughes. He wanted his brother to win. The only way he could guarantee that was for you to lose," one of the sons says.

"It would have gone a lot easier if we'd gotten King out of the way earlier."

"What do you mean?"

"Shut the fuck up," David Duval hisses at the son with the biggest mouth.

"What's the point? We're all fucking dead anyway," the kid hisses back. "This is your doing. Not mine. Not theirs." He looks at each of his brothers, then back to me. "We were supposed to take King out, a few weeks back, but when we sent our guys storming into your old man's house, the fucker was nowhere to be found." He shrugs.

Dad and Vinny had put it down to something else, but it looks like these bastards were behind that attack too. How had none of us seen it before?

My dad hands me a gun, and I crane my neck to peer back at him. "You said you wanted to do it."

I nod and wrap my palm around the grip. "Which one of you fuckers destroyed my daughter's bedroom? Threatened to take her? To hurt her?" I look each man in the eye and have my answer when I get to the third brother, who quickly drops his glare to the ice.

I hold the gun up to his head and pull the trigger. Without thought. Without waiting for verbal confirmation. I don't need it. Then I pass the nine back to my dad and walk away. I don't have to be here for the rest. I got what I wanted. The Valentinos can have at it.

I find myself in the locker room. No idea why I even came in here. Other than out of sheer habit. As I look around, I can feel a shift in the air. Or maybe it's just me? I don't know. What I do know is that things are never going to be the same.

I have a daughter now. I have Kathryn, and there isn't a goddamn thing I wouldn't do for either of them. I sit down on the bench and stare up at the ceiling. I don't regret anything I've done over the past few weeks. That probably makes me a psychopath or something. I would, however, like to just get back to living a somewhat normal life. Don't get me wrong, there's always been an element of danger growing up with my last name. But it's different when that danger's directed at your kid. My kid.

Alessandro comes and sits next to me. He looks around the room. "Finally get backstage access and the players aren't even here," he comments.

"What the fuck do I look like?" I laugh.

"You don't count. I know you."

"Lil never got you inside New York?"

"Nope. She won't let any of us near Travis." He chuckles.

"She probably wants to keep the fucker alive."

"Yeah. Is there any truth to the rumors that the guy is being picked up by the Knights?"

I drop my eyes to Alessandro. I know he's Liliana's little brother, but to anyone who didn't know that, you'd think the fucker was older. "He's been offered," I tell him.

Four gunshots can be heard in the distance, all in succession. And both Alessandro and I look back towards the door while knowing there isn't anything to see from here.

"Guess they didn't feel like playing today," he says.

"Do ya ever get sick of it? The mafia prince life?"

"I don't know anything else. Besides, the perks far outweigh the bullshit." He smiles.

"Yeah."

"You know, I was fourteen... the first time. No one, other than my dad and my Zio Matteo, knows about it. But that first one? It's the one that will stay with you. After that, the rest of 'em just become nameless, faceless pricks. You'll find a way to move past it," he says.

"Yeah. Thanks."

"Where's your uncle been? I haven't seen him around since we got into town."

"Uncle Lou? Dad sent him to Toronto, not long before the playoffs. No idea why." I shrug.

"Huh, they used to be inseparable," Alessandro says.

They did. My Uncle Lou was like my dad's shadow. I'll have to remember to ask Pops what's going on with them later. I've been so hyperfocused on Graycee and Kathryn I haven't stopped to think about it.

Chapter Thirty-Six

Kathryn

I appreciate Gray's family helping Graycee and me. But, boy, am I glad to be getting out of this house. Gray came home two days ago and said we could finally leave. He had to arrange to have some basic furniture delivered and set up first, though.

And today is the day. We're going home. I'm not sure when I started thinking of Gray's place as *home*, but I like it. I feel like a huge weight has been lifted off my shoulders. Like we were always supposed to do this. Be together.

I've never felt lighter, happier. Although, there is still a whole lot of guilt and *I should haves* going through my head. Every time I watch Graycee with her father, I regret not allowing her to experience this sooner. And I wonder if she will hate me for it one day. Right now, she's too young to know it was my fault. But if she ever asks, I will tell her what I did and hope she can find a way to understand or forgive me for it.

I'm still waiting for the other shoe to drop with Grayson, for him to turn around and tell me he doesn't want me anymore. Fairy tales aren't real. They're fables, created so that people like me are forced to dream about happily ever afters. So this— my dream of a happily ever after playing out right before my eyes—feels like a sick joke.

Like, someone out there is saying: *Here, Kathryn. Here's an example of what you could have had. And now that you've experienced it, you'll really know what you've lost when it's all taken away again.*

I don't deserve it, but I will fight to keep it. I

made the mistake of running once. And I'll never do it again. I will do whatever it takes to keep my relationship with Gray. To mend it. I know it will never be what it was back in college. We've both changed, grown during our years apart. But perhaps it can be better. My feelings for him never faded. If anything, they're even stronger now.

"You ready?" Gray asks, stepping into the bedroom with Graycee tucked against his side. For someone who didn't have a father for the first five years of her life, she's really got this whole *daddy's girl* thing down pat.

"More than ready," I tell him.

"Daddy's building an ice rink like Poppy's but bigger," Graycee reminds me while wrapping her arms around my leg.

"Well, aren't you just the luckiest little girl alive?" I take hold of her hand, look up, and smirk at Grayson. "Lead the way, *Daddy*."

His eyes darken as they travel down to my chest and then back up again. "Never in a million years did I think I'd like hearing you call me that. But we will most certainly be putting that to use later tonight," he tells me.

"Sure thing, Daddy. Now, come on. Let's go

before your dad changes his mind and keeps us here," I say.

"I wouldn't put it past him. You know, he offered me fifty percent of the team. If we moved permanently..."

Jacob has been very vocal about how much he'd prefer we just stay here. Raise Graycee in a home where he can see her every day. The man is a girl dad himself. I understand why Grayson's sister is the way she is. Jacob spoiled her rotten too.

"There is no price you can put on privacy. Besides, I don't know about you, but I'm ready to start the rest of our lives. Just the three of us. Until there are four, that is."

Grayson's eyes light up before they drop to my stomach. He's convinced that I'm knocked up already. I'm not. At least I don't think I am. I didn't know I was pregnant with Graycee until I was two and a half months along. I didn't feel sick at all, and whatever I did feel I put down to stress and heartache.

When we get to the front door, Jacob is waiting there. "Are you sure I can't change your mind?" he asks Grayson.

"Sorry, Dad. You can't have my daughter." Gray laughs. "You do remember you have your own, right? The one you're so freely giving to King?"

"You need to let your sister have her happiness, Grayson. You think I don't want to spread that kid all over the ice? Trust me, I do. But I won't be responsible for breaking Aliyah's heart," Jacob grumbles.

"I like him," I add in my two cents, not that it's worth much, and the matching glares I get from both Gray and his dad tell me I'm right. My opinion is better kept to myself. "Or not?"

"I knew you'd come around to my way of thinking." Gray wraps an arm around my shoulder.

"Sure." I laugh.

"Poppy, you don't have to be sad. You can visit me. And I can visit you," Graycee says. She lets go of my hand and hugs Jacob around his legs now.

"Oh, sweetheart, I'm not sad. I'm just gonna miss having you here. This big old house is too quiet without kids inside it."

"Oh, well, maybe you should get some more kids," Graycee offers an easy solution—at least to her, it is.

"Yeah, that's a good idea." Jacob eyes me and Grayson.

"I'm working on it." Gray smirks.

If ever my face were bright red from embarrassment, now is that time. I don't say anything. I mean, what can I say? Grayson just told his father he was purposely trying to impregnate me.

"Okay, I'll let you go, but make sure you bring Graycee around to visit real soon," he says.

"Sure thing," Gray replies. "Thanks, Dad."

I shake out from under Grayson's arm, step up to Jacob, and throw my arms around his neck. I've never hugged this man before, but it feels appropriate now. He stiffens for a second, then his hand reaches up and closes around me.

"Thank you. For everything," I whisper.

"Anytime. If you need anything, you come to me, okay?" Jacob whispers back.

I nod my head and step away.

"Oh, it's new," Graycee says, walking into her bedroom, which still smells like fresh paint.

"You had the walls touched up?" I ask Grayson. The color is the same but the top coat is definitely new.

"I wanted everything fresh for her." He shrugs.

"I love you, Grayson Monroe. Like really, really love you," I tell him.

"Hold that thought," he says, before grabbing my hand and tugging me over to Graycee's new canopy bed. I sit next to him. "Graycee, come here. I have something for you." He pulls two envelops from his pocket, lifts her up, and sits her in the middle of the bed. "I have one for each of you." He passes an envelope to her, then one to me.

"What is it?" Graycee asks.

"Open it and find out," Gray tells her and then looks at me. "Open it."

I tear into the top, reach inside, and pull out a ticket before something else falls onto my lap. A huge something. I pinch it between my index finger and thumb and drop the ticket on the bed. I look up at Gray, who has the biggest smile on his face.

"Grayson? What is this?" I ask, staring at the diamond ring that's blinding me with its sparkle.

"I think it's a ring," he says in that cocky way he does.

"Oh, Disney! Daddy, Disney!" Graycee shouts while waving her ticket in the air after finally managing to pry it free from her envelope.

My eyes flick to the tiny pieces of white confetti at our feet, and I'm surprised she didn't rip her ticket in all the rush to find out what was inside.

"It is! We're going to Disney, baby," Gray says. Then he picks her up and sits her on his lap again. "But first, I need to ask your mama a question. A *very* important question," he adds when his eyes lock on mine.

I swallow the lump in my throat. *Is this really happening right now?*

Gray plucks the ring from my fingers and takes my left hand with his right. "Kathryn Kilgor, you are my one and only love. The kind most people never find, but I found you. Twice. And now I want to keep you. Please tell me I can keep you forever. Will you marry me?"

Graycee glances in my direction. Then looks at her father. And back to me again. "Yes!" she answers for me.

"Shh, this one Mama has to answer, baby," Gray tells her.

"Yes." I nod my head as tears run freely down my cheeks.

"Mama, are you sad?" Graycee asks.

"No, baby. I'm happy. These are happy tears."

Gray slides the oversized rock on to my finger. His hand then wraps around the back of my head, tugging my face towards his. His lips land on mine, and then they pull away far too quickly. "Thank you," he says.

"No, thank *you*. Grayson, you are my one and only love too. And I never want to go another day without having you by my side," I tell him.

"You won't ever have to."

"Can we go to Disney now?" Graycee asks, still waving the ticket with the Mickey Mouse ears printed all over it in front of us.

"Next week, Graycee. We're going to Disney next week. And then, you're going to have to go back to school," Gray says.

"Okay, but Disney first?" Graycee asks.

"Yeah, baby, Disney first," Gray tells her.

I look at the two of them, the two most important people in my world, and my heart couldn't be fuller. Coming back to Vancouver was the best thing I ever did.

I say a little silent thank you to my mom. I know

she's up there watching over me, and I want her to know I'm grateful for everything she did for us. Everything she's probably still doing for us from above.

"I love you," Gray says.

"I love you," I repeat with a huge smile.

Epilogue

A Few Months Later

I hate this. I mean, I fucking love it. It's hockey. But I hate being away from my fiancée and daughter. The first week of training camp is always the hardest. This year, it's torture, because I had to leave them behind.

Things have settled down over the last two months. And we've also *settled* into a routine as a family. Kathryn has even looked into enrolling back in college to finish her degree. She was considering it for a bit, and I pushed her towards taking the dive, with the condition she paid her tuition with the joint account I had set up for her.

She'll start classes again next year. In the meantime, I've made sure she doesn't have to work. I found out she was forced to take on multiple dead-end jobs, to provide for Graycee all those years before we were reunited.

I know I didn't know about our daughter, but the guilt that Kathryn did it all alone and struggled financially still hit me. Hard. That won't ever be an issue again, though. I'll make sure my little family never wants for anything.

"What crawled up your ass?" Luke asks, plopping himself down next to me on the bench.

"You?"

"Fuck off. You look like a lovesick puppy," he grunts.

That has me smiling. I am fucking lovesick and

proud of it too. "I can't wait for that puck to hit you in the heart," I tell him.

"Why the fuck would you want to curse me like that? Man, that's some messed-up shit, bro." Luke shudders at the thought.

"Look at that stupid son of a bitch right there. You think he's not messaging the very girl he's gotten death threats over?" I nod towards Travis.

The guy landed himself in Vancouver without his girl last week. According to Kathryn, Liliana is planning on moving once the season starts. Though something tells me her family will put a stop to that.

"He looks depressed as fuck." Luke sighs and shakes his head. "So does fucking King. All of you lovesick asses look the same. I need some new friends."

"King's just butt hurt that we got a shiny new player who's better than him." I laugh, knowing the bastard hears every word.

Liam lifts his head to look at me, then glances over to Travis. "He wishes," he mutters under his breath before returning his attention to his phone. And probably my sister.

"Yo, Travis. Why you chasing a girl who's gonna get your ass shot one of these days?" Luke calls out.

"I mean, just ask King. That shit hurts like fuck. Or so he keeps saying."

Travis blinks at Luke a few times, then smiles. "Love. Also, have you met Liliana Valentino? If that girl's not worth dying over, I don't know who the fuck is."

"Try to not die. I paid too much for your fucking ass," my father says, making his presence known.

Everyone drops their phones and sits straighter, all eyes on my pops. I follow suit. These meetings might drag on, but they're important. I'm determined to keep that Cup, and the only way to do that is to go out and win it all over again.

Epilogue

Kathryn

I drive up to the gates, which are swarming with press. I have to lean on the brakes so I don't mow any of them down. Wouldn't that just make for a great headline?

Grayson Monroe's Long-lost Baby Mama on Trial for Vehicular Manslaughter.

I'm not sure I'll ever get used to the attention that comes with being that man's girlfriend. To say it's been a media circus ever since Gray did that victory lap with Graycee when the Knights won the Stanley Cup last year would be putting it lightly. There were all sorts of speculations and theories printed about us. Gray ended up sitting down and doing an interview with a reporter, just to set the record straight.

Well, not the entire record. He didn't tell them everything, of course. But he did go public with the fact that Graycee is his daughter and I'm his fiancée. A term I'm still getting used to hearing, even though Gray says it as much as he can.

When I get closer to the gates, they open and I drive through. There are at least fifteen of Jacob's men standing guard. It's not unusual for there to be so many guys here, but this is a little excessive. Even for him.

"Mama, who are all these people?" Graycee asks while staring out the back of the car.

"Reporters, baby. Remember, Daddy and I talked to you about them? They like taking photos of Daddy because he's so good at playing hockey."

"He's the best at hockey," Graycee says. "And so is Uncle Liam."

"Yep, they're both the best," I agree as I park the

car in the garage. I wait for the door to roll back down before I get out.

It's an old habit, from when I was always looking over my shoulder, but now that people are trying to get photographs of my daughter, I make sure I always wait for the added barrier between her and the outside world.

"Come on, let's go find something good to snack on. Then we need to find a good spot for Jasper to spend the weekend."

Jasper is Graycee's class pet, a damn guinea pig. Its beady eyes freak me the hell out, so wherever that thing is living for the weekend, I plan on making sure it's far away from me.

"Jasper can sleep in my room," Graycee says.

I scrunch my nose. "Don't you think he'll stink up your room?"

"Nope, I think he'll be sad if he's alone. I'll keep him company." Graycee jumps out of the car and runs inside, leaving me to collect Jasper, who is staring at me through the bars of his cage with a pair of beady, *judgmental* eyes now.

"Okay, Jasper. It's two nights. We can do this. Just don't die or kill me, and we'll be fine," I tell him.

"Daddy!" I hear Graycee's scream as I enter the house, and my steps increase in speed. Gray isn't supposed to be here. He's just started training camp.

"What's wrong?" I ask as soon as he's within earshot, and then set the cage on the floor.

Gray looks from the guinea pig to me. "I've only been gone a week. You replace me already, babe?" he asks.

"Hardly. That's Jasper, Graycee's class pet."

Grayson wraps his spare arm, the one that isn't holding our daughter, around my neck. Then his lips press to mine. "I've missed you," he says against my mouth.

"Why are you home? You're supposed to be at training camp. What happened?"

Gray sets Graycee back down on her feet. "Baby, can you go get two glasses and the chocolate milk ready? I'm right behind you. I got cookies too."

She runs off in the direction of the kitchen without having to be told twice.

"Gray, what's going on?" You know that feeling, that one that tells you something bad has happened, or is about to happen? Yeah, I have that right now. My heart is pounding. I can hear it in my ears.

"Travis got shot," Grayson says, keeping his voice low.

Also by Kylie Kent

The Merge Series

Merged With Him (Zac and Alyssa's Story)

Fused With Him (Bray and Reilly's Story)

Entwined With Him (Dean and Ella's Story)

2nd Generation Merge Series

Ignited by Him (Ash and Breanna's Story)

An Entangled Christmas: A Merge Series Christmas Novel (Alex and Lily's Story)

Chased By him (Chase and Hope's Story)

Tethered To Him (Noah and Ava's Story)

Seattle Soulmates

Her List (Axel and Amalia's Story)

McKinley's Obsession Duet

Josh and Emily's Story

Ruining Her

Ruining Him

Sick Love Duet

Dom and Lucy's Story

Unhinged Desires

Certifiable Attraction

The Valentino Empire

Devilish King (Holly and Theo's Story)

Unassuming Queen (Holly and Theo's Story)

United Reign (Holly and Theo's Story)

Brutal Princess (Neo and Angelica's Story)

Reclaiming Lola (Lola and Dr James's Story)

Sons of Valentino Series

Relentless Devil (Theo and Maddie's Story)

Merciless Devil (Matteo and Savannah's Story)

Soulless Devil (Romeo and Livvy's Story)

Reckless Devil (Luca and Katarina's Story)

A Valentino Reunion (The Entire Valentino Crime Family)

The Tempter Series

Following His Rules (Xavier and Shardonnay's Story)

Following His Orders (Nathan and Bentley's Story)

Following His Commands (Alistair and Dani's Story)

Legacy of Valentino

Izzy and Mikhail's Story

Remorseless Devilette

Vengeful Devilette

Vancouver Knights Series

Break Out (Liam and Aliyah's Story)

Know The Score (Grayson and Kathryn's Story)

Light It Up Red (Travis and Liliana's Story)

Puck Blocked (Luke and Montana's Story)

De Bellis Crime Family

A Sinner's Promise (Gio and Eloise's Story)

A Sinner's Lies (Gabe and Daisy's Story)

A Sinner's Virtue (Marcel and Zoe's Story)

A Sinner's Saint (Vin and Cammi's Story)

A Sinner's Truth (Santo and Aria's Story)

About the Author

Kylie made the leap from kindergarten teacher to romance author, living out her dream to deliver sexy, always and forever romances. She loves a happily ever after story with tons of built-in steam.

She currently resides in Perth, Australia and when she is not dreaming up the latest romance, she can be found spending time with her three children and her husband of twenty years, her very own real-life, instant love.

Kylie loves to hear from her readers. You can reach her at: author.kylie.kent@gmail.com

Let's stay in touch. Come and hang out in my readers group on Facebook, and follow me on instagram.

Printed in Great Britain
by Amazon